Lady Rample and the Mystery at the Museum

Lady Rample Mysteries – Book Eleven

Shéa MacLeod

Lady Rample and the Mystery at the Museum
Lady Rample Mysteries – Book Eleven
COPYRIGHT © 2022 by Shéa MacLeod
All rights reserved.
Printed in the United States of America.

Cover Art by Amanda Kelsey of Razzle Dazzle Designs
Editing by Alin Silverwood

Dedication

For my cousin Josie whose imaginary wardrobe is a constant inspiration and who always has a recommendation for a good murder. Mystery, that is.

Shéa MacLeod

Chapter 1

Aunt Butty was known far and wide for her cocktail parties. Mostly because they generally involved someone swinging—quite literally—from the chandeliers. This particular party was no exception.

This time she'd hired a proper jazz band led by none other than my paramour, Hale Davis. Hale was devilishly handsome, deliciously American, and could tickle a pair of ivories like nobody's business. Half the women, and a few of the men, were casting lascivious looks his way. He was oblivious. After all, why eat mutton when you've got steak at home? Or something like that.

My name is Ophelia, Lady Rample, and in case you missed it, I'm the steak.

Mr. Singh, Aunt Butty's Sikh butler, was doing the rounds with a tray of French 75s. Not an Aviation, but I had a fondness for them. Ada Price clearly agreed with me as she was the one currently swinging from the aforementioned chandelier, her pale pink bias cut tangled up her thighs and her diamanté hair comb in danger of falling off and dropping into someone's drink.

Ada was closer to forty than thirty, but that didn't stop her shrieking with laughter as her feet dangled just out of the reach of her equally inebriated husband. She kicked out a foot, nearly clobbering him in the process. Good thing her gold and black t-straps were buckled on tight, or it might have ended up flying through a window.

"Darling, do come down from there before you get hurt. Here. I'll catch you." Mr. Price swayed, nowhere near catching her.

Fortunately, my best friend Charles "Chaz" Raynott was on hand to gently move Mr. Price aside and untangle Ada from the chandelier.

"Aren't you a doll," she said, giving him a peck on the cheek and leaving a smudge of carmine lipstick. "Do bring me some more bubbly, won't you?" And she promptly passed out in Chaz's arms.

He shot me a rueful smile, before dragging her over to the gold velvet settee and dropping her on it.

Meanwhile, a contortionist Aunt Butty had met heavens-knew-where had climbed up on the piano and was giving everyone a show. She was really very good, despite flashing her knickers willy-nilly. I couldn't wait to write my friend, Phil, about this. She'd never believe it.

Well, maybe she would. She'd met Aunt Butty after all. In fact, Phil would be here at this party if it weren't for the fact that she was visiting our somewhat mutual cousin, Bucktooth Binky, up North.

You see, when my dear Lord Rample died, his title and rather crumbling estate in Yorkshire went to a distant cousin named Alphonse—Bucktooth Binky to you and me—and I got everything else, which is quite a lot. And that meant Binky and I were often at odds with one another. Philoma Dearling was Binky's cousin on his mother's side—my late husband being from his father's. Phil was a darling, unlike Binky, and she and I had become excellent friends. It was too bad she'd missed the party, but I planned to write and tell her every detail. Especially about the contortionist.

"Oh, there you are, Ophelia." Aunt Butty's best friend, Louise Pennyfather, came puffing up, breathing a bit heavily. Poor Louise was a lovely woman but had the unfortunate resemblance to a horse. Her equally unfortunate habit of talking through her nose didn't help matters. "It's a matter of life and death!"

I eyed her over my champagne coupe glass, Aunt Butty's preferred drinkware for such parties as they were less likely to spill than flutes. Louise, like my aunt, had the tendency to get rather... worked up over things. Drama was their middle name, both of them. "Life and death, you say?" I had my doubts.

"Indeed," she confirmed. She glanced around. "Perhaps we should speak somewhere more privately."

"If you can find anywhere private," I agreed.

Aunt Butty's flat, while generous, wasn't set up for private tete-a-tetes, and my aunt was fond of packing in as many people as possible during her little soirees. Every room was crammed with extremely tipsy partygoers, but unlike my own home, there was no garden to escape to.

Finally, Louise dragged me into the bathroom—which had recently been redone with pink fittings and green wall tiles—and locked the door. "At last, we can be alone."

I almost laughed, but I managed to keep a straight face. "What's going on, Louise?"

"As you know, my husband and I are on the board of trustees for the Museum of Britain."

The Museum of Britain was the largest public museum in the country. Located in the heart of

London, it was dedicated to human history, art, and culture. There was an entire room dedicated to ancient China, complete with lacquered cabinets, porcelain flasks, and jade carvings. Not to mention rich silk robes and ornate swords. Another room held samples of every mineral known on Earth, including a set of emeralds that seemed to glow with an inner fire that took one's breath away.

I'd had no idea Louise was on the board, though it came as no surprise. Most people of our status were involved in such things. I, myself, was on the boards for a couple of charities, though I didn't do much except write letters to important people and donate a lot of funds and attend the occasional board meeting. Dull affairs if you ask me.

"Go on," I urged.

"Well, there has been a bit of trouble recently."

I took a sip of my cocktail. Delightfully fizzy and just a tad on the sweet side, the way I liked it. "What sort of trouble?" How much trouble could a museum get up to?

She took my arm and pulled me further away from the door. I don't know how much farther she thought we could get. We were practically standing in the bathtub.

"A Very Important artifact has gone missing," she whispered. She definitely used capital letters.

"Isn't that a job for the police?" I whispered back.

She looked horrified. "Indeed not. The police aren't suited to this sort of investigation."

Actually, that was exactly what they were suited for. I was about to tell her so, only she continued.

"We are at a crucial juncture in negotiations to borrow a special collection of ancient Mesopotamian art from a private collector. Any whiff of scandal could put us in a precarious position. The police cannot be trusted to keep their mouths shut."

She had a point there. If the police knew about the theft, it would be in every paper before morning. "What do you want me to do about it?"

"Dear girl, I want you to solve the mystery of the missing artifact!"

"She's daft, m'lady. Completely 'round the bend." Maddie neatly placed my shoes in my wardrobe with a shake of her head. "No, best you stay well shot of this."

Maddie was my maid, and a decent one at that, but she had *Opinions*, and she wasn't afraid to share them. Loudly. And with emphasis. Also, her warnings were usually incredibly dire. She had no idea how to look at the bright side.

"Be that as it may, I promised Mrs. Pennyfather that I would visit the museum to look into the theft first thing tomorrow, so please have my navy suit ready. I want to look... businesslike."

Maddie unzipped my gown and draped it gently over the back of the armchair. She handed me a pair of peach silk pajamas edged with lace trim. My favorite pair. I slid them on, feeling exhaustion overtake me. As fun as the party had been, I was more than ready for bed.

"Nothing good will come of this, mark my words," she warned dourly, tucking back a lock of dark hair that had escaped the severe bun she'd shoved it into.

"Noted."

She sighed heavily. "I suppose Mr. Hale will be home late."

"Likely."

"I'll put out a sandwich and coffee for him, shall I?"

I tried not to wince, but I'm not sure I was successful. Maddie was an excellent maid, but a terrible cook. She could make an excellent pot of tea and a decent coffee, but her sandwiches were often terribly dry and uninspired. Fortunately, Hale had no problem doctoring up his sandwich to make it more palatable. "That sounds lovely. Thank you, Maddie."

She nodded and pulled my navy Elsa Schiaparelli suit out of the wardrobe. "I'll have this pressed for you tomorrow morning. But don't say I didn't warn you." She shook her head and tutted as she exited the room, taking her little black raincloud of doom and gloom with her.

Bless her, but the woman saw demons lurking in every shadow. There was nothing to worry about. It was just a museum. It wasn't like there were dead bodies lying around.

Chapter 2

"And this is the mummy of Pharaoh Senusintehf. We dug him up in Egypt last year. Marvelous, isn't he?" My tour guide beamed at the glass case which housed a dead man wrapped up in bandages and looking a bit worse for wear what with being ripped from his place of rest and shipped to England to be displayed for all to see. Poor thing.

"Oh, yes, marvelous," I echoed. I owed Maddie an apology, at least in my mind. There actually were dead bodies lying about.

The Museum of Britain sat neatly back from Great Russell Street like a Grecian palace of knowledge. It was glorious to behold, but the true treasure lay within. I was particularly fond of the Egyptian Room, and I wasn't alone in that. Although I could have done without the crusty pharaoh.

"Now over here you see an excellent example of—"

"Listen, Mr. Evans," I interrupted. "I'm meant to be meeting with the head of the museum, Sir John Forsdyke. It's of the utmost importance."

Evans took off his glasses and polished them fastidiously with his handkerchief before pushing them back on the bridge of his beaky nose which sat prominently in a too-narrow face. He was probably somewhere near fifty with a drastically receding hairline, pasty skin that had never seen the light of day, and eyes set just a little too close together. His suit was pressed within an inch of its life. He brushed nervously at his lapel as if trying to remove an invisible bit of lint or dust. "Yes, rather. Well, you see... he's unfortunately unavailable at the moment."

I raised a brow. "Unavailable? I took time out of my day to assist him in an urgent matter."

"Yes, of course, my lady, but... well..." He took my elbow and gently guided me to a quiet part of the exhibit, away from visitors. "He's out of town, you see."

I blinked. "Out of town? After an artifact has gone missing? I understand it's a truly important piece. Why wouldn't he be here?"

Mr. Evans leaned in closer and whispered, "He doesn't know."

"He doesn't know?" I repeated. "Obviously you do, and so does Mrs. Pennyfather. How is it the head of this museum doesn't?"

He sighed heavily. "I'd originally approached Mr. Pennyfather about the situation after I discovered the theft. He promised to look into it straight away, but when I didn't hear from him, I contacted Mrs. Pennyfather and, well, here you are. I'd really rather keep this under wraps, if you don't mind. The only people who know about this are the trustees, and they're not interested in the public knowing about this anymore than I am."

"Very well. Let's get to it, shall we? No more of this faffing about. There's important work to be done if we are to find this—"

"Please, my lady." He glanced around and lowered his voice. "We mustn't refer to the, ah, issue. We don't want to upset anyone." He glanced left and right as if people were hiding behind statues and stelae to listen in on our plans.

"Right. Of course not. Heaven forbid." My tone may have been a touch sarcastic, but I lowered my voice obligingly. "In any case, perhaps we could get on with it? I'd like to begin my investigation."

He shifted uneasily, tugging on the lapels of his inexpensive gray suit. "We're waiting for another party."

"Another what?"

"Here he is." Mr. Evans beamed as a gentleman approached us.

He was tall and fit with thick, blond hair and pale blue eyes and a nose that was slightly on the long side. He was perhaps ten years older than me, and handsome in a proper British way, if you liked that sort of thing. Frankly, he'd nothing on Hale, but then I may be a bit biased.

"My lady, please meet Mr. James Woodward. Mr. Woodward, Ophelia, Lady Rample." Mr. Evans beamed broadly.

I glanced in confusion from Mr. Evans to James Woodward and back again. "And what has Mr. Woodward to do with this investigation?"

"I'm the investigator," he said, handing me his card.

I glanced at it.

> *James Woodward, Solicitor*
> *Woodward & Woodward*
> *Solicitors*
> *London, England*

He was a solicitor? What had that to do with investigating the theft at a museum?

"I assure you, you are not. I was hired directly by the trustees," I said.

"Ah, my lady," Mr. Evans interrupted. "I'm afraid that's not quite correct."

"Excuse me?" I turned to shoot him a glare.

"You were hired by Mrs. Pennyfather." Evans' cheeks pinkened. "The rest of the trustees agreed to hire Mr. Woodward. He has some experience in these matters."

"And I have not?" I drew myself up to my full height of five-foot-five and did my best impression of lady-of-the-manor. "I will have you know I have solved many such cases."

"Which is why I asked the trustees to allow us to work together," Woodward said soothingly.

Frankly, I wanted to take his soothing manner and stuff a sock in it. Instead, I gave him a forced smile. They wanted us to work together? We would see about that. "Very well. Lead on."

Mr. Evans must have sensed the tension in the room, for he gave us a pained smile before turning and leading us through the exhibit out into a hallway to a staircase. It was narrower than most of the others, with a plain handrail and wooden treads instead of marble. Our shoes thumped on the treads, echoing in the stairwell as we made our way to the upper floor.

"The goddess statue was on display in the Special Collections Room," Mr. Evans said as we finally arrived on the top landing. His cheeks were ruddy from the climb, and he seemed a little out of breath. Evidently, he didn't get up here often. "It's a little out of the way, but it's an intimate room, perfect for small collections. This way."

"Can you tell us a bit more about the statue?" Woodward asked.

"Yes, yes, of course. The statue is of an unnamed goddess dug up in the Middle East some years ago. Unlike most such statues which are made of clay or bronze, this one was covered in gold, lapis lazuli, and red jasper. Very unique and of incredible value. It's been in a private collection and is only on loan." He shook his head. "We do not need the owner finding out about this."

The Special Collections Room was the last door along the hallway. Before we entered, I pointed to the window at the end of the hall. The ordinary wooden sash was painted plain white, the glass frosted. "Where does that lead?"

"A side street, actually. Nothing terribly interesting," Evans said. "Hence the frosted glass. The view is rather ugly."

"It's marked as a fire exit," James spoke up. "Perhaps the thieves could have got out that way."

Mr. Evans shushed him. "Please. Wait until we get in the room."

The room itself had a rope barricade out front with a sign marked *"Closed for maintenance."* Evans moved the barricade aside and unlocked the door, then let us in before replacing the barrier and shutting the door behind us.

The room was much more intimate than most at the museum, only about twice the size of my sitting room. The wood floors were highly polished, pendant lights hung from the high coffered ceiling, and the walls were painted a rich lapis lazuli blue. No doubt that had been done to highlight the goddess statue. There were no windows in the room, no doubt to prevent fading or whatnot from sunlight.

Mr. Evans led us to a chest-high cherrywood pedestal in the middle of the room. On top sat a glass case over a velvet draped stand which currently was empty. "This is where the goddess statue was displayed. As you can see, while it is gone, nothing else in the room has been touched."

I glanced around. Sure enough, the matching cherrywood cases around the room were filled with all kinds of interesting artifacts, many of them gold or bejeweled: masks, torque style necklaces, bracelets and bangles, statuettes. Nothing seemed to have been disturbed.

"How tall is the statue?" I asked.

"About ten inches," Mr. Evans said, indicating the height with his hand.

"All right, tell us exactly what happened," James demanded as he prowled the edges of the room as if the object in question might have been mislaid in one of the corners. He even poked in the garbage bin that was set near the entrance.

I tried not to roll my eyes to the heavens and only succeeded with some difficulty. He was making quite a show of it.

"It was early in the day, not long after we opened, and it wasn't terribly busy yet. A young woman approached one of the guards and informed him she'd come to see the goddess statue specifically and was outraged that the room was closed for maintenance. Since this room was not scheduled for maintenance, the guard came straight to me, and I went to check it out. I found the goddess statue missing and the glass case on the floor. I put it back since I didn't want it to get damaged."

"And nothing else was amiss?" James asked.

Mr. Evans shook his head. "Not a thing."

"Was the door opened or closed?" I asked.

Both men stared at me like I'd suddenly grown a second head.

"We always leave it open for visitors during the day," Mr. Evans said. "All the rooms are."

"But was it open or closed when you arrived?" I tried not to let my exasperation show. "You mentioned that the young woman said it was closed for maintenance."

Mr. Evans' eyes widened. "The door was closed but unlocked. Most definitely. And the *Closed for maintenance* sign was hung on the knob which is *not* how we do things."

"And nothing inside was amiss except for the missing statue?" James pressed.

"Yes, as I said." Mr. Evans' tone was a little stiff. "I immediately locked the room and told the guards to search everyone who left the building. They did, but no one had the goddess statue."

"Could they have left the museum prior to the alarm being sounded?" I asked.

Mr. Evans shook his head. "Doubtful. Another of the guards had just done his rounds prior to the discovery, and the room was open and all as it should be. The thief or thieves would have had less than ten minutes to escape. And while a few people did leave, the guards said none carried bags large enough to contain the item, nor did they wear bulky clothes that would have allowed them to conceal it."

No doubt the thief—or thieves—had expected they'd have more time. Although obviously ten minutes had been more than enough. Still, it seemed too short a time to steal the artifact and get through the museum without being noticed.

"Is there an exit they could have left by that isn't guarded?" James demanded.

"The employee entrance," Evans admitted. "Only it's locked. You need a key to get in or out, and none of the employees left during that time."

"You searched them, too, I suppose," I said casually. "And their offices or lockers or whatnot?"

He nodded. "Of course."

That ruled that out then.

James Woodward strode from the room without a word. Evans and I exchanged a glance before following him. He headed straight for the window at the end of the hall and shoved it open. It was one of those sash ones that had to be hoisted above one's head. He leaned out, then back in, shaking his head.

"They didn't get out this way. It's a sheer two-story drop. They'd have broken a leg."

"How is that a fire escape?" I asked.

"There's a rope ladder in the box there along with a fire axe," Mr. Evans said with a flush. "We plan to put in a proper escape ladder, but it hasn't been a priority."

In other words, whoever was donating money wanted it spent somewhere flashier than a metal ladder. Never mind it could save lives.

"This window… was it open?" James barked.

Mr. Evans shook his head. "It was closed and locked, and the ladder was still in its box. They definitely did not go out that way."

Which took us back to square one. How did a thief steal a priceless artifact in the middle of the day and escape without being seen?

Chapter 3

Once he'd finished showing us the scene of the crime, Mr. Evans lead James and me back down the stairs to his office on the ground floor. It was on the small side but with high ceilings and an equally tall, narrow window that let in plenty of light. The desk was a simple, modern affair situated to face the door with an oil painting of a man in early 18th century garb hung on the wall above. If it was meant to be impressive, it was, and perfectly suited the curator of a museum.

He motioned us to the two seats obviously meant for visitors before lifting the receiver of his black phone and barking, "Gladys, tea." I couldn't help a slight frown. Apparently, his dubious charm was reserved for those he considered his betters.

Mr. Evans kept up a banal string of pleasantries, barely allowing us to get a word in edgewise, until Gladys appeared with the tea tray. She was young and pretty and giggled a bit as she passed 'round the teacups, fluttering her lashes at James Woodward.

"That will be all, Gladys," Mr. Evans snapped.

She scurried out of the room, head down, shutting the door behind her. I was about to reprimand him for his ill behavior toward the young woman, but James started speaking before I could get a word in.

"So this goddess statue, what's the background? Why's it all hush-hush?"

Mr. Evans reached into his desk and pulled out a set of photographs which he handed over—to Woodward of course. Fortunately for the good of both men, Woodward gave the pictures a quick perusal before passing them over to me. The first two were of the statue from various angles. There were three more: one of the dig where it was found, one of it in situ, and one of a dandily dressed gentleman posing with it like it was a war prize.

"It was dug up in Iraq over two decades ago by Sir George Smithers. That's him there in the last photo. Quite the find. Never seen anything like it. Sir George was sure he was onto something."

"On to what, exactly?" I asked.

His eyes glittered with something. Excitement? Avarice? "The mythical city of Aratta."

James and I both stared at him blankly.

He sighed. "Aratta was supposed to be home to the goddess Inanna, a fabulously wealthy placed filled with gold, silver, lapis lazuli…" He nodded toward the photograph of the goddess statue. "Basically, that sort of thing. The city appears in various pieces of ancient Sumerian literature, but so far, no such historical place has been found. Everyone thought it was a myth until Sir George dug up that statue. He was sure he was close, but then the Great War came along and put a stop to it. Haven't been able to put spade to earth since."

"That's a shame," I murmured. "Imagine what else could be found there." I enjoyed history and archaeology, mostly because of the mystery behind things. I did love a good mystery. No doubt that was why I'd stumbled into so many over the years.

"It is, indeed," Mr. Evans agreed wholeheartedly. "So much yet to be uncovered, but here we are, twiddling our thumbs. In any case, Sir George has kept the statue in his private collection all this time. He sadly passed on last year, and his heirs agreed to loan us the statue for display."

"Again," Woodward prodded, "what makes this object so valuable?"

"Seriously?" I stared at him like the moron he clearly was. "It's covered in gold and jewels."

Mr. Evans all but tutted. "As I said, it is a rare find. Setting aside the historical value—which is immeasurable—monetarily the item is so rare that there are private collectors that would pay a fortune—a very large fortune—for such an artifact."

I made a moue. In my opinion, rich people who bought up historical artifacts and stashed them away so no one could see or study them were utterly contemptable. That was a level of greed I just couldn't get behind. Historical items like the goddess statue belonged to the world, not one man. Bad enough they were dragged from their country of origin and stashed in museums, although at least they could be studied, I supposed. And anyone who wanted to could come and see them in a museum.

"I understand that," James Woodward said, "but what I still do not understand is why, other than a minor dent in your museum's reputation, do you feel the need to hide the theft? Surely the police are better equipped to handle such an investigation."

At least he and I were of like mind on that.

"Minor dent?" Mr. Evans all but shrieked. "Reputation is *everything* in this world. Many of our exhibits are on loan from other countries or private collectors. We depend on donations from wealthy patrons to keep this place running and sponsor archaeological digs around the world. If word got out we'd had an artifact this important stolen from under our noses, no one would ever again loan us their collections. We'd hemorrhage donors left and right! It would be an utter disaster!"

He was being overly dramatic, I thought, but I could see his point of view. Reputation *was* everything. Particularly to the upper crust who seemed to think even a whiff of scandal would mean the end of civilization. Personally, I thought a bit of scandal now and then did a body good, but then I was considered a bit on the scandalous side myself. Someone like Aunt Butty or me or even Louise Pennyfather wouldn't pull our donations—as long as there were assurances made that there would be improvements to security and such—but plenty of others would. And he was right about the loans. I couldn't begin to imagine that any sane person would loan a valuable collection of art or artifacts to a museum with a reputation for losing them.

"Had the artifact been on display long?" I asked.

Mr. Evans shook his head. "Barely over a week. In fact, it wasn't supposed to have been displayed until next month, but the owners suddenly demanded it be returned sooner than agreed upon which meant we had to put it on display early. Up until then, it had been downstairs for cleaning and examination. We always want to study and learn as much as possible about our artifacts before putting them on display."

"Let me guess," Woodward said dryly, "several people examined it."

"Well, of course everyone on the team wanted to get a look at it," Evans admitted. "Plus a few who aren't. It's such an unusual item."

"I doubt the thief was anyone who spent much time with the artifact," I said.

Both men turned to stare at me.

"Why is that, my lady?" Woodward said with excruciating politeness.

"Because," I said with equally excruciating patience, "if it were one of them, they could have easily swapped out a fake for the real thing at any time and no one would have known the difference. They are the experts after all. They could have lied."

Both men looked a bit non-plussed. I tried very hard not to smirk.

"However," I continued, "that doesn't mean it wasn't an inside job. I'd like to speak to anyone who worked on the object."

Mr. Evans hesitated.

"Yes," Woodward spoke up. "I think that's a splendid idea."

"You're right, Mr. Woodward. Jolly good!" Mr. Evans leapt from his chair as if it had been his idea all along.

I nearly rolled my eyes. Men.

I'd never seen the working side of a museum before, and I found it incredibly fascinating as Evans led us through various departments, describing what we saw along the way. In one room, a reedy man was pouring white goop into a mold of some kind.

"What's he doing?" I asked with interest.

"Ah, he's making dinosaur bones," Mr. Evans said.

"*Making* dinosaur bones?"

"Well, yes. You see, the real bones are far too valuable to be put on display. They could be damaged. Some are extremely fragile. So we make plaster casts and age them to look exactly like real bones. Or at least close enough from a distance." He winked at me, then blushed as if realizing who he was winking at. He cleared his throat. "Anyway, yes, bones."

From there, he led us into an even larger work room where several people were bent over a massive length of cloth. Each of them had a magnifying glass and seemed to be going over the object with a fine-toothed comb.

"This is where we clean and repair some of our more delicate artifacts such as the tapestry you see there."

Ah. That explained the length of cloth.

We wound our way through what seemed like a warren of various rooms and hallways. I supposed there was a more direct route, but he clearly wanted to give the full tour. Perhaps he hoped I would make a contribution.

Eventually we passed through a massive storeroom with shelves crammed full of boxes and stacks of crates covered in sheets. There were long tables set up among the stacks, similar to those we'd seen in the work rooms. No doubt to allow museum personnel to study the items stored in the room. Currently, however, the place was empty, and our footsteps echoed hollowly.

Finally, he led us to a long hall with doors on either side, most closed. One stood open, and he directed us there to the small room far in the back where a woman about my age—which is to say somewhere in her thirties—was hunched over a table, magnifying glass to one eye. A small, black stone statuette sat on the table mere inches from the glass, a lamp shining on it. She didn't even look up when we entered, focused entirely on the statuette, muttering to herself as she jotted notes in a black leather notebook.

Mr. Evans cleared his throat. "Miss Pierce?"

"Go away, Evans, can't you see I'm busy?" By her accent she wasn't British, but from America. Her hair was a plain medium brown with a few grays shot through, about shoulder length and held back by a simple tortoiseshell clip. She wore a white lab coat over a plain linen blouse and a pair of stylish wide trousers. And she clearly had no time or patience for our host.

He sighed heavily. "This is important, Miss Pierce."

Her sigh was even heavier. "Very well." She set down the glass and leaned back, giving us the once over. She immediately dismissed James Woodward, but her gaze lingered on me. "Well, at least there's someone intelligent in this crowd." She muttered it, but loud enough for us all to hear.

Mr. Evans harrumphed. James laughed. I just gave her a knowing look.

Mr. Evans made quick introductions. The whole time, Miss Pierce looked bored, more interested in her artifact than her visitors.

"This is Mabel Pierce. She works on cleaning and restoration of artifacts. Miss Pierce, this is Ophelia, Lady Rample and Mr. Woodward. They're here to investigate…well… You know, the *incident*…"

When he finally stumbled to a stammering halt, she tucked a lock of stick straight hair behind one ear and picked up her magnifying glass. "If you're finished, Evans?"

He flushed. "It's *Mr.* Evans."

She shrugged. "I'm busy."

"This is important," he wheedled.

"He's right. It's important," I said, deciding to take pity on the man. "It's about the goddess statue that was stolen."

She set the glass down again and straightened back up. "Well, why didn't you say so?" She turned to face us. "I'm surprised the idiot told you the truth."

Mr. Evans turned bright red and spluttered out a bunch of unintelligible nonsense. I was rather liking this Miss Pierce.

"Evans tells us you worked on the object, Miss Pierce." Woodward took over as if he were in charge. Much to his chagrin, Miss Pierce completely ignored him.

Instead of answering his question, she directed her next words at me. "Ophelia, is it?"

Evans blanched. James Woodward cleared his throat. I could care less if she used my honorary. I knew from experience Americans were much more casual about forms of address than the British, and I rather liked it.

"Indeed, Miss Pierce."

"You can call me Mabel." She slid off her stool and walked over to me, hands tucked in the pockets of her white coat. "Like the man said, I worked on the goddess statue before it went on display. They only let me clean it up. Forget I'm an expert in ancient Mesopotamian artifacts. I've probably forgotten more than most of them will ever know, but it's a man's world." She sneered.

"Don't I know it," I murmured. It must be beyond frustrating for a woman as intelligent as Mabel to be stuck doing menial tasks when she had more expertise than anyone else in the department. "What can you tell me about the statue?"

She shrugged. "It's a rather stupid thing to steal."

"Why's that?" James asked sharply.

She slid him a look then turned back to me. "There are hundreds, if not thousands, of items in this museum that are unremarkable yet valuable and easily hawked."

"Not the goddess statue, though," I guessed.

She shook her head. "I mean, the value is... inestimable."

"It's invaluable," Evans piped up.

She closed her eyes as if in pain. "Yes, Evans, that's what I just said. It's also unique and incredibly rare. One of a kind, actually. It would be difficult to find a buyer. It would pretty much have to be a very wealthy private collector. Someone who knew the artifact could never see the light of day."

"Because if they did, it would immediately be spotted as stolen," I mused.

She nodded approvingly. "Honestly, in my opinion, the greatest value is what we can learn from it. It really should have been examined much more than it was. But no, it *had* to be put on display." She shot Evans a glare. "Where it was promptly stolen."

"Not my fault," he said, holding up his hands. "I had orders."

She let out an indelicate snort.

"You don't think the thieves will be able to sell it?" I asked Mabel.

"Unlikely, unless they've got a line on a buyer already. No one else would touch it. Too hot."

"Perhaps they already have contacts in the artifact collector world," I mused.

"Very clever." She smiled. "That was my thought."

"Not really," I said. "It's a simple matter of deductive reasoning."

James Woodward gave me a long look but didn't say anything. Unlike Evans, he struck me as a man who also had deductive reasoning and likely could follow my pattern of thinking.

I was beginning to think this was likely an inside job.

Chapter 4

I left the museum shortly thereafter without much more clarity than I'd entered. Somehow someone had smuggled the goddess statue out of the museum without anyone the wiser, and for purposes that might or might not be nefarious. What a pickle.

I climbed into my Mercedes Roadster—which my late husband Felix had bought for me brand new in 1931 and which I hadn't the heart to sell as it was still far and away my favorite vehicle—and headed home, my mind admittedly more on the mystery than the drive home. I wasn't sure what steps to take next. According to Evans, there were a couple of scholars who'd inspected the stolen artifact, but neither of them had been available for questioning. Which seemed suspicious to me. Evans had known I was coming—and James Woodward, too, apparently—and yet hadn't bothered to ensure the two men were on hand? I couldn't decide if the man was stupid or just incompetent.

Or perhaps he was far cleverer than I gave him credit for.

I shook my head as I veered around a corner with a screech of tires. Unlikely. He'd have to be a marvelous actor.

I pulled up with a lurch outside my townhouse and hurried up the walk, deep in thought. I had the men's names—a Dr. Prentiss and a Dr. Foster. I could track them down. I'd have to play my cards right, though. No doubt they wouldn't take kindly to being questioned by a lady detective.

I all but snorted aloud. Look at me, calling myself a lady detective. How ridiculous. Solving mysteries was nothing more than a hobby of sorts. It wasn't like I went looking for crimes to solve. They just sort of... found me.

My husband, Felix—may he rest in peace—had once said I had the mind of a terrier. Once I got my teeth into something, I wouldn't let go. I'd never been entirely sure he'd meant that as a compliment, although I chose to take it as one.

The front door swung open before I could even stick my key in the lock. Maddie stood in the entrance, her aquiline nose nearly quivering in outrage.

"My lady, you have guests." Her tone was nothing short of accusatory.

"Why didn't you tell them I wasn't at home to visitors?" I said, brushing past her into my entry hall. There was a vase of fresh pink tulips on the sideboard. From Hale no doubt.

Maddie all but rolled her eyes. "They're not the kind of visitors a body can say no to, if you get my meaning."

"Ah, Aunt Butty and Louise," I said as I unbuttoned my lightweight blue short jacket that matched my suit.

"Got it in one, m'lady."

"And Hale?"

"Still abed. He got in shortly after you left for the museum."

Hale and his band were currently billed at the most popular jazz club in London, The Rhythm Club. They often played until the wee hours, staying on even after the club closed to eat together and play casually. What Hale called a "jam session." It wasn't unusual for him to come home after I was already awake and going about my day.

"We'll try and keep it down, then," I said, handing her my coat, then turning to the hall mirror to unpin my hat.

Something crinkled in my pocket. With a frown, Maddie reached in and pulled out a crumpled half sheet of lined paper and handed it to me. "What's this, m'lady?"

"I've no idea." I took the paper and unfolded it. It was a note, handwritten with bold strokes in graphite pencil. I recalled Miss Pierce had been using such a writing utensil when we'd visited her. I quickly scanned the note.

Ophelia,

I'm surprised that idiot Evans told you the goddess statue was stolen. He has hidden at least 2 other thefts of which I am aware. Meet me at midnight in my lab. Side door open. Will discuss more.

Mabel Pierce

"Well, isn't that interesting," I murmured.

"What is it, m'lady?" Maddie asked.

"A clue to my latest investigation, I hope," I said, refolding the note and tucking it into my dress pocket. "How about some tea?"

She sighed heavily as if she were quite put upon. "Very well." And she plodded away.

Repressing a laugh, I entered my sitting room where Aunt Butty and Louise—along with her dog, Peaches—had made themselves at home. Aunt Butty had clearly been in my liquor cabinet as they were drinking scotch and sodas while flipping through my collection of fashion magazines and gossiping about someone or other whose daughter was trying to land an earl.

"There you are, dear girl," Louise said. Only it came out "gel" instead of "girl." She fluttered a hand at me. "Have you found the thief?"

"Hardly," I said, taking a seat at the other end of the sofa. "I only just met with Mr. Evans today. Louise, did you know the museum has hired someone else to investigate?"

Her expression turned grim. "Unfortunately, yes. I only found out this morning. Certain members of the board wanted a man on the case." She lifted her gaze to the eaves as if praying for strength.

"My dear Ophelia," Aunt Butty said, "you do know that you can never trust a man when it comes to these things. They can be very obtuse."

I lifted a brow. "I'm fairly certain there's an entire police force that would disagree with you." Although based on some of the members of said police force, Aunt Butty may be on to something.

She snorted in an unladylike manner. "Be that as it may, it doesn't change the facts. You do remember some of those we've had to deal with over the years. Like that ghastly North fellow. If it weren't for us, why, prisons would be overflowing with innocent people."

She was exaggerating, of course. Though she wasn't entirely wrong. Detective Inspector North had been a thorn in my side on more than one occasion, arresting people on zero evidence, based mostly on his personal biases, only to discover later they'd nothing to do with the crime. He'd even once arrested yours truly. Fortunately, I've friends in high places, or it might have gone very badly for me. I shuddered to think what happened to people without my resources.

"Be that as it may, I am forced to deal with the man."

"What man?" Aunt Butty asked, getting up to refresh her drink.

"James Woodward," I said. "He's the one the museum board has hired to officially investigate."

"I've met this Woodward once or twice," Louise said. "Handsome and very charming when he wants to be. And not entirely stupid."

"A glowing recommendation if ever I heard one," I said dryly.

Maddie interrupted before Louise could reply, entering the room with a tea trolly piled with treats. "Don't worry, my lady, I didn't bake the cake," she said, bringing the cart to a jarring halt. "I got it from your favorite bakery."

Thank goodness for small miracles. Maddie was not a great cook, though she made an excellent pot of tea and rather edible toast.

While I poured tea, being hostess and lady of the house, Maddie handed 'round generous plates of cake and scones with cream and preserves.

Louise poked at the brown cake with a frown. "Dear girl, what do you call this monstrosity?"

"Banana cake," Maddie said calmly, completely unruffled by Louise's horror. "It's quite the thing, apparently. All the greengrocers are passing out recipes so as to use up old bananas."

"*Old* bananas?" Louise paled.

"There is a depression on, you know," Maddie said tartly. "I tried one. It's delicious."

Louise harumphed. "We'll see about that."

Apparently, she decided she liked it because, after declaring that it was no lemon cake, but it would do, she ate three pieces. Aunt Butty was right behind her. As for me, I never met a cake I didn't like.

While we enjoyed our tea, I told the older women about my visit to the museum, along with how the goddess statute had disappeared without a trace despite there being no easy way to get it out of the building. I also gave a quick rundown of my conversation with Mabel Pierce. "I'm meeting her tonight at the museum. I think she has more information for me, but she didn't want to say anything in front of Mr. Evans."

"Or Mr. Woodward," Aunt Butty pointed out.

"I doubt he's involved in anything nefarious," Louise said. "He always struck me as a solid sort. Very law abiding."

"I don't mean that he's behind anything illegal," Aunt Butty said. "Just that perhaps as a woman, Miss Pierce felt uncomfortable speaking in front of men."

I very much doubted that. Mabel Pierce had struck me as the sort of person to speak her mind regardless. No, it was much more likely that whatever she had to tell me had to do with the theft of the goddess statue—not to mention the other missing items she'd mentioned in her note—and there was someone in the museum who was involved. Someone she didn't want to know she was cooperating with the investigation.

Question being, was it Mr. Evans? Or was it someone else? Either way, I'd be meeting with her tonight and hopefully get to the bottom of this.

Chapter 5

It was dark out as I pulled my car to a stop on a poorly lit side street. The museum loomed dark and almost ominous above me, the streetlamp on the corner giving off only enough light to cast long, eerie shadows and not much more.

A few feet away, steps led down from the pavement to where another light glowed above a door. This was the employees' entrance which James and I had inspected earlier. The one that could only be opened with a key. I hoped Mabel had left it open as she promised.

I climbed out of my car and took a good look around to ensure I wasn't watched. The street was completely empty. If anyone was hiding in the shadows, I couldn't tell. Although why anyone would be lurking about after dark was beyond me. Well, besides myself, of course.

Shoulders back, I strode briskly to the stairs, taking the half dozen steps down and grasping the doorknob. At first, I was afraid the door was locked, but then I realized someone had jammed a bit of paper into the mechanism to prevent it from doing so. Clever. No doubt Mabel's work.

I cautiously let myself inside. The lights were off, the hall nearly pitch black save for a spill of light from a room at the other end. I was fairly certain that was Mabel's office from what I remembered of the layout.

Try as I might to move quietly, the leather soles of my shoes made a light tapping sound against the tile that echoed down the hall. I winced. I should have taken my shoes off, although it would have been a pain to unbuckle them. So much for being subtle. I was surprised Mabel didn't pop her head out and chide me.

I realized once I reached the lab the reason was that she wasn't there. The lamp on her desk was on—that was the light I'd seen—her pencil and notepad out as if she'd been working on them. Her handbag and tweed polo coat still hung on a coat tree in the corner, so she must be around somewhere.

Unsure what to do, I waited, but after a few minutes I began to feel restless and fidgety. Where was Mabel? Why would she not be here when she'd been the one to ask for this meeting? Something was off. I just knew it.

Stepping out into the hall, I peered into the darkness, but could make out little. I knew the door was behind me and, recalling my earlier tour, there was that large open storage room in front of me. Could she be in there? And if so, why not turn on a light?

"Miss Pierce?" I called out. "Mabel?"

There was no answer. Only silence. Not even a shout from a guard. Probably more concerned about protecting the exhibits than ensuring the safety of the employee areas.

It was so dark, I wished desperately I'd brought a torch, but who would have imagined I'd need it in a museum? Particularly one to which I'd been invited.

I hesitated in the doorway. Mabel had said to meet here, but she was nowhere to be seen. Should I wait longer? Or go in search of her?

I decided to wait. After all, she could have simply gone off to use the facilities or grab a cup of tea and would be back any moment.

Still, as the minute hand moved around the clock, the bad feeling that had been niggling at the back of my mind grew exponentially. Something was wrong here. I was certain of that.

Finally, after a good fifteen minutes, I'd had enough. I was going in search of Mabel!

I exited Mabel's office and stepped into the large storage and work area, closing my eyes to allow them to adjust. When I opened them, I realized that the cavernous space wasn't as dark as I'd first thought. Faint light from the streetlamps outside streamed in through high windows, turning the pitch black into more of a dark gray. The massive stacks of crates were inky shadows against the dark background. On the other side of the cavernous space, I could make out a faint bit of light that must be coming from the main museum.

It took a while to cautiously pick my way around the crates. I stubbed my toe at least twice in the process, but at last I came to the door that led out into a hall which led to the stairwell up to the museum. It, at least, was unlocked, and the lights were on. With a sigh of relief, I pushed my way through the doors and took the steps to the lobby. There should be a guard I could speak to.

Only there wasn't. The lobby was dimly lit and eerily empty. The moonlight diffused through the glass dome soaring high above glowed against the white marble floor and created thick shadows along the edges of the room where Corinthian pillars supported the edges of the dome. I knew that between those pillars were archways leading to various exhibits, but they were all dark. Save one.

A light shone from one of the display rooms. Perhaps Mabel was in there. Or the guard, at least. I strode quickly across the lobby.

It was the Egyptian Room where I'd met Mr. Evans earlier that day. Bas reliefs and sections of brightly painted tomb walls lined the room. The floor space was taken up by looming pharaohs carved in stone, granite obelisks blasted by sand and time, and elaborately decorated wooden sarcophaguses, some with mummies still inside. To say it was eerie was, perhaps, an understatement. A shiver ran up my spine as if someone had just walked over my grave.

As I rounded a massive edifice of an ancient pharaoh, I stumbled to a halt. For there, draped across one of the highly decorated sarcophagi, was the body of Mabel Pierce.

Shéa MacLeod

Chapter 6

"Who are you?" A voice boomed from behind me. "What are you doing here?"

I whirled to find a guard striding toward me. He was a large man, one of those who'd once had muscles but had now gone mostly to fat, with a round face and a thin mustache. He wore a museum uniform which strained at the seams, and his expression was one half of worry and half of outrage.

"My name is Ophelia, Lady Rample, and I've been hired by the museum curator, Mr. Evans. Come quickly. I think Miss Pierce has been harmed."

"What?"

Ignoring him, I raced over to where Mabel was draped over the sarcophagus, then hesitated. It was clear that she was likely beyond any help I—or anyone else—could give her. A jewel hilted dagger protruded dramatically from her chest, although there was surprisingly little blood.

"What the devil?" The guard staggered to a halt beside me. "Is she—?"

I closed my eyes a moment, inhaled, then opened them. "Let me check her pulse." Not that I wanted to—I was almost certain of what I would find—but it seemed the thing to do. And the guard was a bit... unsteady. Since his breath could strip paint off the walls, I was certain he'd been spending more time in a bottle and less guarding the place.

He frowned. "You know how to do that?"

I gave him a look. "I was a nurse during the war."

Something like respect flitted across his face and he nodded. "Right. Go on then."

I reached out and laid two fingers across Mabel's wrist as it dangled over the edge of the sarcophagus. Her skin was cold—too cold—and as I suspected, no pulse. I shook my head. "I'm afraid she's dead."

He blanched. "What happened?"

"I don't know. I had just found her when you came in."

He gave me a suspicious look. "What were you doing here?"

"As I said, Mr. Evans hired me to do some work here at the museum." I wasn't sure if the guard knew about the theft, though I supposed he must. Still, I didn't want to blab anything I shouldn't. "I had an appointment to meet with Miss Pierce after hours. When she wasn't in her office, I decided to look for her."

I'm not sure my explanation appeased him entirely, but he looked somewhat less suspicious of me. "I need to ring Mr. Evans. He should know about this."

"And the police," I said.

He nodded. "Yes. Of course. You'll wait here?"

I shrugged. "I have nothing else to do at the moment."

His eyes narrowed. "Don't touch anything."

I nearly rolled mine. "Of course not." What was that quaint American phrase? "This isn't my first rodeo."

He gave me a funny look, then hurried off to use the phone. No doubt he thought I was one of those daft aristocrats with half my brain missing. Ah, well. I didn't mind people underestimating me. Made my job easier. I often found I could use such things to my advantage. Easier to poke around and uncover secrets when no one suspected you had more than two brain cells to rub together.

While he was gone, I carefully inspected the scene. It was, in a word, overly dramatic. As if the killer had wanted to make a statement. The dagger looked to be something out of the exhibit, overly decorated and not particularly useful. However, if it really was ancient, the blade would have likely snapped during the attack. Not a good murder weapon. Also, I didn't recall seeing the dagger in the display during my tour earlier that day. My guess then was that it was a reproduction and not in fact the real thing.

The lack of blood was curious. If she'd been killed here, there should be plenty of blood, which there wasn't. Not to mention, since she was cool to the touch, she'd been dead since long before the museum closed. I doubted the museum patrons would have forgotten to mention a dead woman in the Egyptian room. She was likely killed elsewhere and dragged here after the museum closed. Why? If it was simply for dramatic effect, the killer had certainly accomplished their goal.

A quick glance around revealed a floor that was sparkling clean. No blood trail, so either the killer had time to clean up, or she'd been killed here and there'd simply been less blood than expected. Which was possible as there was only a single stab through the heart. The dagger itself had prevented any major blood loss.

I was about to get a closer look at the body when I heard the rumble of voices from outside the room. Not wanting to be caught leaning over the crime scene, I stepped back a few paces.

Shockingly, Mr. Evans arrived before the police. He still wore his nightshirt but had managed to put on pants, a jacket, and shoes, although one was brown and one was black. His hair stood on end, and his eyes were round in his pale face.

He staggered into the Egyptian Room. "What happened?"

I gripped his shoulder to stop him from touching the body. "I'm sorry, Mr. Evans, but Miss Pierce has been killed."

His mouth opened and shut. "Killed?"

"Murdered," I said. There was no doubt of it. It certainly hadn't been natural causes. Knives don't go sticking themselves into people's chests, generally speaking.

He turned even paler and swayed so that I was half afraid he'd topple over. "M-murdered? How is that even possible? Why would anyone kill Miss Pierce? There must be some mistake."

"No mistake, sir." The guard made his way around a statue of Ramses the Something—I couldn't recall which one, not that it mattered at the moment. "Lady Rample here found her. Checked her pulse. She's definitely dead, sir."

"But why?" Mr. Evans wailed. "And why here in the Egyptian Room? It's our most popular room."

Was he really worrying about that right now? Mabel was dead!

"You called the police?" I asked the guard.

He nodded. "Unlocked the front door so they could get in. They should be here—"

There was shouting and a clattering of feet out in the lobby.

"—now," he finished lamely.

Within moments, the Egyptian Room was swarming with uniformed officers. One hustled me to the side. I can't say I was impressed with his manhandling.

Then through the door came a face I had hoped to never see again. The man was completely average in looks to the point of being forgettable. He was of medium height, medium build, and medium coloring. Even his rumpled suit was a medium gray. Only his eyes were memorable, staring out at the world with a cold hardness that chilled to the bone.

He stopped in front of me, a sneer crossing his face. "Well, as I live and breathe. Ophelia Rample."

I sneered right back at him. "It's *Lady* Rample to you, Detective North." Not that I cared about titles, but his lack of respect for me as a person irked.

He gritted his teeth. "It's Detective *Inspector*."

I shrugged. "Potayto, potahto."

Red tinged his cheeks, and his eyes snapped with anger. North had never appreciated my involvement in his investigations. Particularly because he had a bad habit of accusing innocent people of crimes, and I had the habit of proving he was wrong. He should have thanked me for saving his lazy backside, but instead, he just got more miffed every time we crossed paths.

"What are you doing here, Rample?" he snapped.

"I had an appointment, North."

"With?"

I pointed to the dead woman sprawled across the sarcophagus. "Her."

He glanced at the body and let out a heavy sigh. "Why is it that every time you're around, there's a murder nearby?"

"Just lucky, I suppose."

His eyes narrowed. "I'm told you found the body."

Oh, dear. Here we went again. I'd bet my last coin he was about to accuse me of murder. "I did. Which makes me your prime suspect, I suppose, but before you get out your manacles, I can assure you I am quite innocent."

He crossed his arms. "Really?"

"Indeed. First, here is the note Mabel sent." I dug in my handbag and handed him the slightly rumpled missive. "I arrived promptly as requested. You can speak to Maddie my maid and she will confirm when I left the house. I arrived here at the museum less than half an hour ago. As you can no doubt tell, Miss Pierce's body is cool to the touch. Which means it's been at least twelve hours since she was killed. At that time, I was having tea and banana cake with my aunt and her friend, Mrs. Pennyfather."

His eyes widened slightly. I'd figured he'd recognize the name. Not only was Louise on the board at the museum, but her husband did something hush-hush for the government. I'd never been sure exactly what. I'm not sure anyone knew, even Louise.

"Also," I continued, "as you can no doubt tell, the body has been moved—"

"How can you tell?" he interrupted. "Unless, of course, you were involved."

"Don't be daft. There is no way on God's green Earth that I could have got a corpse onto that sarcophagus. I don't have the upper body strength. I know she was moved because while there is blood on her body, there is none on or below the sarcophagus. If she'd been murdered here, there'd at least a small pool. Not to mention, she was likely killed around noon. You cannot convince me she was killed in the most popular room in the museum, and no one bothered to mention it."

"You're right," he muttered reluctantly. "At least about moving the body. Although you could have done it with help."

I gritted my teeth. "If I didn't kill her, then I'd have no reason to move her, would I?"

He grimaced. "I suppose not."

"In fact, you know very well I am not a killer or even the killing type. I think I've helped you enough to earn a little trust, don't you think?"

He grimaced. "You're a civilian, Rample. Don't push it. You may go for now."

I shook my head in exasperation and turned to leave.

"Lady Rample?"

I whirled back and snapped, "What is it, North?"

"Don't leave town." His expression was equal parts grim and smug.

I gave him my cheeriest smile. I really should have listened to Maddie. "Oh, don't you worry, detective. I wouldn't dream of it. No, I think I'm going to stay right here, close at hand." I let my gaze drift to the crime scene and then back to him.

I swear the man blanched.

Chapter 7

By the time I arrived home, I was wide awake. Instead of going to bed, I rang up Chaz and begged him to come over.

"You're lucky," he informed me when he arrived, dressed neatly in a black suit, a white button-down shirt, and a silk ascot in peacock blue. "I had nothing to do tonight."

"No fancy parties?" I teased, letting him in quietly so as not to disturb Maddie. She was grumpy if she didn't get enough sleep.

"Well, I had supper with Charles Laughton and a couple of other people."

"Goodness! Don't tell Aunt Butty. She'll be back to writing screen plays for you to foist on the poor man," I said.

Chaz laughed. "In any case, it was such a dull affair I nearly nodded off. All he could talk about was this production company he's founding with some German fellow. It was so dreadful, I actually went home early. You have saved me from myself. Cocktail?" He sauntered over to the drinks cabinet.

"Yes, please."

"What'll it be? Highball? Martini?"

"Aviation, darling. What else?"

"Coming right up."

As he mixed together gin, creme de violette, and other delightful things, there was a pounding on the front door. Since Maddie had gone to bed hours ago, I answered it myself, surprised to find James Woodward on my doorstep, dressed to the nines in a tuxedo and top hat as if he'd been to the opera or some such.

"You do realize this is the middle of the night?" I said coolly.

"How dare you go snooping around the museum!" The "without me" was clearly implied.

I grinned. "You're jealous I didn't invite you."

If he'd been one of those little Walt Disney cartoons, steam would have come pouring out his ears. "I don't think you understand how dangerous this situation is."

"Oh, don't be a drip," I said. "I know very well how dangerous investigating crimes is. I'll have you know I've solved several murders in my time. Now instead of standing on my doorstep, shouting like a fishmonger, would you like to come in? My friend, Chaz, is fixing drinks." Without waiting for an answer, I turned and walked back to the sitting room. "You can toss your coat over the banister. Hat, too."

I guess Woodward decided the only option was to follow me. He carefully shut the door behind him. I was impressed he didn't slam it. He certainly was steamed enough. Then he divested himself of his outerwear before joining me in the sitting room.

Chaz was giving the cocktail shaker a vigorous shake when we entered, the ice rattling noisily against the metal sides. He gave Woodward a slow once over. "Well, hello. Who do we have here?"

"Chaz, darling, this is James Woodward, thorn in my side. The museum board hired him to investigate the missing goddess statue I told you about."

"I thought they hired you for that."

"Louise hired me. Apparently, the rest of the board thinks only a man will do." I turned toward my guest. "Mr. Woodward, this is my dearest friend in the world, Charles Raynott the Third."

"Call me Chaz, old man." Chaz reached around to give Woodward a firm handshake. "Just mixing up drinks. Would you like one? Of course you would!" He didn't wait for an answer but poured the periwinkle-colored liquid from the shaker into two coupe glasses and handed them to us before refilling the shaker for himself.

Woodward stared from Chaz to the glass in his hand and back again, a befuddled expression on his face. "I'm not here for a drink."

Chaz waved him off. "You're here. Drink up! More where that came from."

Woodward sputtered a little. I found it amusing that the buttoned-up solicitor was so shaken up by a little cocktail. Or maybe it was Chaz. Hard to say, but I held back my grin and steered him to the sofa.

"Please, have a seat and we can talk about this like civilized people."

He joined me, taking a sip of his cocktail. He grimaced.

Chaz caught it and lifted a brow. "Something wrong?"

"Sorry," Woodward muttered. "Bit sweet for my taste."

"Here." Chaz snatched it from him and took it to the cart where he stirred in more gin and lemon juice. "Now try."

Woodward took a cautious sip, the raised a brow. "Quite nice. Thank you."

Chaz lounged in the chair across from us. "What can I say? I know my drinks." He gave

Woodward a long, meaningful look which the other man either didn't catch or pretended to ignore.

I'd seen Chaz show interest in men before, but he seemed keener on Woodward than usual. Interesting. Whether Woodward returned the interest was hard to say. If he did, he didn't know me well enough to let his guard down. If he didn't, I hoped he didn't rat Chaz out. I constantly worried my friend would find himself in trouble with the law, which didn't take kindly to men who preferred the company of other men. It was why I was so protective of Chaz and often attended parties with him. Not only was it fun, but it kept him safe. I'd have to keep a close eye on Woodward. If he hurt my friend, he'd be the one with the jeweled dagger in his chest.

"Listen, my lady—"

"Just call me Ophelia," I said. "I'm not into that 'my lady' business."

"Except when it suits her," Chaz muttered.

"Very well. Ophelia." Woodward cleared his throat. "If you'll call me James." His gaze slid to Chaz, his expression definitely warmer than when he looked at me. "Both of you."

Chaz grinned, and I felt myself relax. I had nothing to worry about, at least when it came to Chaz.

"You were about to chew me out?" I nudged.

He grimaced. "I apologize, I meant no such thing, but I have... concerns."

"Go on."

He shifted. "If we are to investigate this thing as a team, we need to do these things together."

I lifted a brow. "You think I can't take care of myself?"

"I've no doubt you can," he admitted. "You have a certain... reputation."

I grinned. "I know. Ain't it grand?"

He chuckled. "The point being, I need to know all the information you know to be able to question all the players. And I need to be able to watch your back as well as have you watch mine."

"As long as I am privy to your information as well," I said.

He nodded in agreement. "Fair enough. Now, why were you at the museum?"

I sighed. "When we were there yesterday— was it yesterday already?" I glanced at the clock. "Yes, yesterday. Mabel Pierce slipped a note in my pocket. My maid found it when I got home. In it, Mabel asked me to meet her later that night in her lab. That she had more to tell me."

"Can I see this note?" he asked.

"Sorry, the police took it. Fortunately, I have an excellent memory." I winked. "In the note, she claimed that more than one item had been stolen from the museum in the recent past, but that Mr.

Evans had hidden that fact and she would tell me more when we met." I shrugged. "Unfortunately, that was all."

He sat back in his chair, a thoughtful expression on his face. "And when you went to meet her?"

"The employee entrance was unlocked as she promised. The light in her lab was on, but there was no one there. Although her possessions were. I waited for some time, and then went in search for her. I assumed that perhaps she was visiting the lady's or some such. Only I found her... dead in the Egyptian room, a dagger in her heart."

"That's rather dramatic," Chaz said.

"My thoughts exactly," I agreed. "Even more dramatically, she was draped over one of the sarcophagi on display."

James leaned forward. "But why did you go to the Egyptian Room in the first place?"

I frowned. "I'm not sure."

"Think back," James urged. "What was it that you saw or heard that drew you there?"

I closed my eyes a moment and pictured the ominous darkness of the storage room. "The light. I followed the light?"

"What do you mean, old girl?" Chaz asked eagerly, his drink forgotten.

I opened my eyes. "The lights were all off except in Mabel's office. That big storage and work area beyond was completely dark. Other than the office, the only light I could see—dim as it was—came from what I thought was the lobby. Only when I got to the lobby, I realized the lights were off there, too. It was the lights in the Egyptian room I'd seen. I thought it was strange that those would be on while the rest of the museum was dark, so I went in there, and I found Mabel as I described."

James grimaced, shaking his head. "I'm sorry you had to see that."

"Had to see what?" a rich, melodious voice asked from the drawing room doorway.

We all turned to stare. A man leaned there, one shoulder pressed to the frame, his full lips curled up in a slight smile that had far more heat in it than was appropriate in mixed company. His broad shoulders filled out his suit rather nicely. His skin was a rich, deep brown, and his dark hair, cut close to a well-shaped skull, was pomaded so that it held only the tiniest bit of curl.

An answering smile crossed my face. "Hale, darling. You're home! How was the club?"

"Good turnout," he said, strolling over with his hands in his pockets to lean down and give me a kiss. "Three curtain calls."

"Marvelous," I said. "Of course they love you."

"Drink, old man?" Chaz asked, getting up before Hale had a chance to answer. "It's Aviations tonight. Unless you want something else?"

"An Aviation is fine." Hale turned toward James. "And this is?"

"Oh, sorry. This is James Woodward. Remember I told you about him. James, this is my paramour, Hale Davis."

If James was shocked by my calling Hale my paramour, he didn't bat an eyelash. Instead, he rose and gave Hale's hand a vigorous shake. "Call me James, Mr. Davis. You're American?"

"Hale, please. Mr. Davis was my father. And yes, I'm from New York originally, although I spent many years in New Orleans." His grin turned lopsided in that adorable way it did. "And yes, love, I remember you said Woodward was a sniveling jackanapes."

James sputtered, and Chaz burst out laughing.

"Spineless jackanapes," I corrected. "And that was before we agreed to work together."

"I see. Thanks," he said to Chaz, taking the proffered drink. "And what is it that you had to see that was so terrible?"

"She found another body," Chaz said, refreshing his own drink before taking a seat. "Par for the course, really."

Hale let out a heavy sigh before perching on the arm of the sofa next to me. "Really, Ophelia? Another?"

"Another?" James lifted a brow.

"She's found more than her fair share, and that's a fact," Chaz said. "Always coming across mysteries, our Ophelia. It's like we can't go anywhere without stumbling over a corpse."

"That's hardly fair," I muttered.

"Perhaps not," Chaz admitted. "But it's true."

"He's got you there," Hale agreed, giving my shoulder a squeeze.

I sighed. "Very well. I do seem to have some sort of... special ability in that arena. But it's hardly my fault."

The two men in my life scoffed. Poor James Woodward just looked bemused.

"Who was it that you found this time?" Hale asked.

"A woman who worked at the museum. Mabel Pierce. I was supposed to have a meeting with her, only... Well, she was already dead when I got there."

Hale didn't say anything but reached down and squeezed my hand. I swallowed. Only Hale truly understood that sometimes being faced with death so often got to me. However, I took solace in the fact that, more often than not, I was the one who brought the perpetrator to justice. With the help of my friends, of course.

"Perhaps you could leave this one to the police," Hale suggested.

"I can't. James and I were hired to solve the mystery surrounding the museum's missing goddess statue, and somehow Mabel's death is tied into that. I'm sure of it."

"As am I," James agreed. "But I promise to look out for her."

I scowled at him. "I can look out for myself, thank you very much."

"Never hurts to have someone at your back," Chaz pointed out.

"Watching your six," Hale agreed.

James leaned in. "I watch your back, you watch mine. Deal?"

I considered him a moment before nodding. "That is a deal I can get behind."

"Excellent," James said. "Now what do you think our next step should be?"

"Can you find out if the police found anything in Mabel's lab?" I asked, knowing he had connections I didn't.

"Already done," he said. "According to my source, they found nothing of interest. However, they found a smear of blood in the storage area that someone tried to clean up. They believe that's where she was murdered. Since the lights were off, you wouldn't have seen it."

"I'd like to go back and search Mabel's office," I said. "Perhaps there's a clue there. Something the police missed."

James nodded. "We'll go together."

I started to rise, but he held up his hand. "In the morning—later in the morning, that is—when we're both rested and fresh."

I sighed. He had a point. "Very well." I rose. "I'm to bed. Chaz? You'll see James out?"

He slid a look at James then back to me. "Of course. Sleep well, darling."

As Hale followed me up the stairs, I heard Chaz say, "Another?"

"Don't mind if I do." James' voice was a low rumble.

I smiled to myself. I had a feeling James would be anything but well rested in the morning.

Chapter 8

Sure enough, James Woodward met me at the museum the next morning looking a little worse for wear. His eyes were bloodshot, he wore the same shirt and trousers he had at my house—though he'd swapped out the tuxedo jacket for a regular suit jacket—and his hair was a bit ruffled. I barely held back a smirk.

"Go ahead, laugh," he grumbled.

"I guess you and Chaz got on."

"We sat up for hours talking. He's an interesting fellow. Very... charming."

"Yes, he is. He's also my best friend." I let the warning note linger in my voice. Nobody messed with Chaz if I could help it.

He gave me a long look. "In my line of work, it pays to be discrete. To hold confidences. And to keep one's friends safe."

"Then we understand each other."

"Indeed."

I nodded toward the museum entrance. "Now, let's get in there. We've got a murder to investigate."

"Don't you mean a theft? The murder is the police's business."

"And if we happen to solve a murder while solving a theft, what can we do?" I held up my hands. "Just doing our jobs."

He laughed. "Well, come along, Miss Marple."

"I'm hardly old enough to be Miss Marple," I said tartly, following him up the wide, shallow steps.

"No, but you're certainly nosy enough," he muttered.

"I'll take that as a compliment."

The guard on duty recognized us immediately and greeted us by name. He'd a brass name badge that read: Boyle.

"Are Dr. Prentiss and Dr. Foster in, Mr. Boyle?" I asked.

"Yes, my lady, they are. Do you need to speak with them?"

"Yes, please," I said. "And then we'd like to see Miss Pierce's office, if you'd be so kind."

"Of course. This way." He led us back into the employee area. Both the storage area and Mabel's office-cum-lab were roped off as crime scenes but there were a few lights on in other offices and labs. "That there is Dr. Prentiss' lab. And you'll find Dr. Foster in his office. Down that hall, third door on the right."

"Thank you, Mr. Boyle," I said with a smile.

He bowed, reminding me a little of Mr. Singh, before returning to his duties.

"Let's tackle Prentiss first."

James nodded. "Lead the way."

Turned out, Prentiss was the gentleman I'd seen making plaster casts of dinosaur bones on my first visit to the museum. He was currently perched at a worktable, magnifying glass in front of one eye, peering at what appeared to be an overly large vertebra.

"Dr. Prentiss?" I asked.

He glanced up, looking momentarily confused, as if he wasn't quite sure where he was. He smoothed a hand down his white lab coat and offered a half smile, glancing from me to James and back again. "Uh, hello. Do I know you?"

"Ophelia, Lady Rample. And this is my business partner, Mr. James Woodward. We were here the other day. You were making a cast of one of the dinosaur bones."

James gave me the side-eye, but I ignored him. After all, we were partners of a sort.

"Oh, yes. Pleased to make your acquaintance. Elton Prentiss." He slid off the stool and walked over to shake our hands. His grip was limp and his skin smooth and a bit damp. He seemed… nervous.

"Your specialty is paleontology?" James asked.

"Yes, indeed. Specifically the Late Cretaceous period." At our blank looks, he clarified. "The time when the great Tyrannosaurus rex roamed the Earth."

"Ah," I said, as if that cleared things up. I doubted I could tell one dinosaur from another, to be honest. "Mr. Evans said you were one of the specialists who studied the goddess statue before it was stolen."

"Yes, I did. Quite a stunning piece," he said.

"Bit late for you, isn't it?" James asked.

Prentiss blinked. "What do you mean?"

"He means it's a bit odd, a paleontologist studying an Ancient Mesopotamian artifact, isn't it? Not really your specialty," I said.

"Ah, that." He rocked back on his heels. "You're right, it's not. It was… curiosity more than anything. The goddess statue is a unique find, unlike anything else from that era. Mabel wouldn't shut up about it, so I went to have a look."

"You and Mabel were close?" James asked.

He shrugged. "Not really. Just colleagues. She could be a bit… annoying. All this women's suffrage nonsense. Always yelling about how the museum wouldn't fund her research simply because she was a woman."

"You don't think that was the case?" I asked, trying very hard not to punch his smug face.

"That was no doubt part of it," Prentiss admitted, "but the truth is, there are a lot of politics in the museum. If you don't make nice to the right people, you don't get funding. And Mabel was not one to make nice to anyone."

He certainly had a point there. While she and I had gotten on fine, it was clear that she hadn't been interested in getting along with the men in the room. Not that I blamed her. Evans had been incredibly condescending.

"When did you last see the statue?" James asked.

Prentiss mulled it over. "Two days before it was stolen. I stopped by Mabel's office. Aaron—Dr. Foster—was already there. Ancient Mesopotamian art is his specialty. He was over the moon with that statue. Anyway, I stopped by, had a quick look, made appreciative noises, then left to get back to work."

"And you didn't see it after that?" James asked.

"Afraid not. Didn't even really think about it until I heard it was stolen."

"How did you hear about the theft?" I asked. I knew that Evans had been trying to keep the incident hush-hush.

"Oh, it got around. Trust me, something like that goes missing in broad daylight, and you hear about it. I don't recall who I heard it from first, but both Mabel and Dr. Foster got in a row over it."

James frowned. "Why?"

"Foster accused Mabel of stealing it to fund her research." Prentiss snorted. "For all her faults, I don't buy it. She was protective of the artifacts in her care. There's no way she stole that statue."

"And Dr. Foster?" I asked. "Would he steal it?"

"Unlikely. The man is totally about the science. Money isn't his thing."

"Did you have anything to do with the theft?" James asked.

"Of course not." He reared back, clearly offended. "I like money as much as the next person, but it's not worth losing my job over."

"Even though the statue would have brought a small fortune?" James asked.

"Large fortune," Prentiss corrected. "And no, there isn't any amount of money that would tempt me to leave my dinosaurs." He stroked the vertebra on the desk in front of him, a light of passion in his eyes that was almost creepy. The guy really loved his old dinosaur bones.

"And Mabel's murder? Do you know anything about that?" I pressed.

He shook his head. "I only heard about it this morning when I arrived. Poor kid. She was a royal pain, but no one deserves that."

We thanked Prentiss and turned back toward the hall where the offices lay. James shoved his hands in his pockets, a frown creasing his forehead.

I turned to him. "Do you think he's telling the truth?"

He sighed. "I honestly don't know. Everything he says seems reasonable, but I can't help but wonder why a dinosaur guy would be interested in a goddess statue."

"One made of gold and jewels," I reminded him. "One that is by all accounts incredibly valuable. People have done worse for less."

"True," he admitted. "Let's see what Dr. Foster has to say."

Dr. Foster was in his office, head bent over a book. Where Prentiss had been tall and thin, Foster was short and plump with neatly trimmed goatee and small round spectacles. He looked up with a vague smile when James rapped on the open door.

"Dr. Foster?"

"Yes."

"I'm James Woodward, and this is Ophelia, Lady Rample." He stepped inside, and I followed.

"Ah, yes, the ones Evans hired to investigate the theft of the goddess statue."

"You know about that?" I asked, surprised. I had thought Evans was keeping our investigation quiet.

"My dear, it's very hard to keep secrets in such a place as this," Foster said with a chuckle. "It's much like a village in that way. Everyone knows everyone's business."

"I get that," I said. "I grew up in a small village called Chipping Poggs."

His eyes widened in delight. "I grew up not far from there in Barton Abbots!"

"Lovely village," I said. "I remember enjoying their summer fetes."

"Marvelous good fun those were," he agreed. "Always looked forward to the fetes. But you're not here to reminisce, are you?" His gaze turned shrewd. "No doubt you want to know where I was when the statue was stolen and all of that?"

I smiled. "Very perceptive, Dr. Foster. Let's start with the last time you saw the statue."

He leaned back and clasped his hands over his round stomach. "Two days before the theft. I was studying it in Mabel's office. Masterpiece, that. So unique."

"Dr. Prentiss said he stopped by for a look," James offered.

Foster frowned. "Yes, yes, I recall that. Seemed odd, the dinosaur bone fellow showing an interest in my specialty, but I always encourage curiosity. Keeps the mind sharp. At any rate, I was there for an hour or so, discussing Mabel's findings. Neither of us was thrilled it was being rushed on display. So much more study to do. I argued against it vehemently, but Evans insisted."

"Do you know why?" I asked.

He shrugged. "Money, no doubt. It's always money. The museum is free, of course, but patrons pay extra for the special exhibits. The owners of the statue wanted it back sooner than originally agreed upon. Evans probably figured he could make a tidy sum off people wanting to see the statue before it was returned. And the museum always needs funds."

Made sense, I supposed. "So the last time you saw the statue was that day in Mabel's office?"

"Yes, indeed. I'd planned to visit it in situ, but it was taken before I had the chance." He scowled. "I'd like to get my hands on those thieves. Greed. Sheer greed. No thought to what we could *learn* from such an artifact."

"Did you have anything to do with the theft?" James asked bluntly.

"Of course not." Foster seemed offended we'd even asked. "Nor did I kill that poor woman. I know some around here disliked Miss Pierce, but she was a hard worker and very knowledgeable. She was a credit to our field of study."

"Someone claimed that you accused Mabel Pierce of stealing the goddess statue," I said.

He snorted. "I very well did not. She was the most painfully honest person I ever met. She wouldn't steal a paperclip, let alone that statue."

After thanking Foster for his time, we headed down the hall to Mable's office. James eyed the police barrier across the door. His hesitation made me roll my eyes.

"Come along," I ordered. "Can't allow a little police tape to stop you." I ducked underneath and entered Mabel's office, turning to give a triumphant smile.

He let out a sigh and ducked under as well. "You do realize I am considered to be a law-abiding citizen."

"I won't tell if you don't," I said. "Too bad we didn't get much out of the doctors. Do you think they're telling the truth?"

"Well, one of them is obviously lying about Foster accusing Mabel. Though why Prentiss would make up such a lie is beyond me," James mused.

"Maybe to throw off the scent. Put our suspicion on Foster instead of himself. I'm not sure I trust Prentiss, though I couldn't say why. Just a feeling I get." I glanced over at the now empty coat rack. "Looks like the police took Mabel's handbag and coat, more's the pity."

"Too bad. I'll have a chat with my contact, see if they found anything of import."

I nodded. "That would be good. For now, you start on that side of the room, and I'll look through the desk." In my experience, the desk was the best place to find clues and such. Which is naturally why I chose it for myself.

It didn't take long for me to come across something of interest in the top drawer of her desk. Tucked away at the back under a jumbled pile of paperclips and thumbtacks was an index card. Scribbled on it in graphite was the word "spare" and affixed to it with cellophane tape was a single key.

"I think I found her house key," I said, peeling the tape off the card and holding it up. "It says 'spare' on the card."

"Could be a spare for the museum," he mused. "Lots of doors and whatnot around here."

"Could be," I admitted. "Could even be a spare for her office." I shook my head. "No, that's ridiculous. Why would she keep a spare key to her office inside her office? Wouldn't do her much good if she locked herself out."

"Let's try," he said, plucking the key from my hand and striding to the door. As I suspected, the key didn't fit. "Could be for another lock somewhere else in the building."

"The only other place would likely be the employee entrance. Mr. Evans said that only himself and the guards have the keys to anything else. Let's finish in here and then we'll try it."

"Good idea." He went back to searching the bookshelves while I turned my attention back to rifling through the desk.

"Look here," James said, pulling a simple spiral notebook from the shelf of books along the back wall. It looked like the one she'd been working on the other day. "This appears to be notes on her work."

"Take it. There could be something important in there."

"The police would probably have taken it if that was the case," he pointed out.

"Maybe or maybe not. One book among several others wouldn't stand out. It's the perfect hiding place for something like that, right in plain sight." I held out my hand.

He handed me the notebook with a shrug and went back to inspecting the bookshelves. I tucked the notebook in my handbag and continued rifling through the desk.

If there had been anything else, the police had taken it. All I found were office supplies and files on various objects Mabel had studied. It seemed that while her official job was to simply clean artifacts, she'd taken it upon herself to carefully study and notate anything she considered of interest, including sketches and even photographs of the items both before and after cleaning. These files didn't appear to be official so much as for her personal use. I showed one of them to James.

"There should be a file on the goddess statue. She said she cleaned it, and we have confirmation from both Prentiss and Foster that she was working on it, but there's nothing here. Could the police have taken it?"

"I'll find out," he said, jotting a note in a little black book similar to what I'd seen the police use. "What about the other missing items?"

I shrugged. "No idea. In her note, she never said what other items went missing, so it's impossible to tell."

"I think we need to have a talk with Mr. Evans about these missing items," he said.

"I agree. And we need to ask him if he told the police about them, too. Then we can check Mabel's files against those items. If the files are here, then great. But if they aren't..."

"Then maybe the killer took them," he finished.

"That's my thinking." I tucked the files neatly away. They'd been alphabetized and clearly marked. Mabel had obviously been a stickler for detail. Hopefully it would help us. "Let's go find Mr. Evans."

Unfortunately for us, Mr. Evans' secretary informed us he was under the weather and was taking the day off. I certainly found that strange.

I asked her if she knew anything about the artifacts that had been stolen from the museum. She either didn't know anything or wasn't going to admit to it. In any case, she had nothing of interest to impart.

"That's convenient for him," I muttered as we exited the museum and walked around to the employee entrance. "One of his employees is murdered and he's suddenly taken ill?"

"Not everyone has your constitution, Ophelia," James said with some amusement, taking the key I held out.

"No, that's true. Thanks for noticing." I winked.

He laughed as he inserted the key into the lock and gave it a twist. It didn't turn. "Guess it's not for this lock. Let's try a few more."

We reentered the museum where we tried several locks before giving up, including every office in the hall as well as a couple of nearby storage room doors. It was a bit like looking for a needle in a haystack.

"If the key opens anything in this museum, it isn't a lock easily found." I shook my head. "In fact, I'm beginning to think whatever it opens is not in his building at all."

"Let me guess," James mused as we once again exited the museum, "you want to see if that key belongs to Mabel's flat."

"Indeed, I do. And I assume you have her address?"

"Of course."

"Then lead on, MacDuff."

"You know that's a misquote," he said wryly.

"Of course I do," I said. "But the misquote makes much better sense, don't you think?"

"I try not to," he muttered.

Mabel lived not far from the museum in a flat above a pub. A green door next to the pub entrance led into a narrow hall that was dim and smelled of cooked cabbage and old ale. A door to the left led into the pub while a flight of rickety steps led up to the next floor.

The stairs creaked heavily as we made our way up to the landing, off of which were two doors, each to a flat. The one facing the front and the road had the number 1 painted on the door while the one to the back had a 2. The 2 was Mabel's flat.

I slotted the key into the door, and it turned like a charm. "Ta-da! I told you!" I crowed.

"So you did."

I swung open the door, but before we could step inside, a dark figure barreled out the door, crashing into me before dashing down the steps. James immediately went after him, not even stopping to see if I was alright.

I was, fortunately, save my dignity. And I appreciated a man with correct priorities. Unfortunately, he came limping back.

"He got away."

"Dash it all!" I scowled. "Did you get a good look at him?"

"Unfortunately not. He wore a muffler that covered most of his face."

"In this weather? He must have been roasting to death." It was a warm day, not unbearably so, but certainly too hot for a muffler. "Nothing for it. We must press on."

We stepped inside. The place was in an absolute shambles.

The flat was a one bedroom with built-in shelves along one wall and a tiny kitchenette in an alcove. Every book had been tossed from the shelves onto the floor. Plants had been uprooted from their pots, the dirt in piles everywhere. Sofa cushions had been sliced open, stuffing poofs scattered about. In the kitchenette, every cupboard door stood open, the pots and pans inside half falling out. And the bedroom was a disaster with the mattress half off the bed frame and clothing strewn everywhere.

"Do you think our intruder caused this mess?" I mused.

"Most likely. While the police aren't known for cleaning up after themselves, they don't typically cause this big a mess."

"True. I've seen North's handiwork in the past. It's bad but not this bad."

"Have you? Chaz said you'd solved a few mysteries. I assume that's when you came into contact with Detective Inspector North?"

"Oh, yes. He and I have butted heads on more than one occasion. He's always wrong, by the way. Although he probably took anything even resembling a clue," I said with a sigh as I glanced around the flat.

"Maybe, maybe not." He glanced at me. "Steady, old girl. Don't give up on me now."

I snorted. "If you knew me better, you'd know I never give up. In fact, it's been said of me that I go where angels fear to tread."

He lifted an eyebrow. "Really? And who said that?"

"I believe it was Chaz." I gave the disheveled room another look. "Shall I start in the bedroom area?"

"Very well. I'll check out the kitchenette." As we made our way to our respective corners, he cleared his throat. "So, speaking of, what's the deal with your friend Chaz?"

I slid him a look. "What do you mean?"

"Is he, ah, involved with anyone?"

"Not currently. That I know of."

"No wives or fiancés or such?"

"Definitely no wives." I wasn't about to break Chaz's confidence to a near stranger, even though I suspected there was no issue with James. "And his last relationship, such as it was, ended when we left Paris a few months ago. I don't believe there's been anything even vaguely serious since. Why do you ask?"

He cleared his throat. "You don't know me—"

"No, I do not." I opened the drawer on the bedside table, but all the contents had been dumped already.

"And I don't know you, but I know of you."

"Do you now?" I glanced over to find him standing there, an empty teapot clutched in his hands.

"And what I've heard is that you are a woman of honor with an open mind and a closed mouth when it comes to those you... care about." His expression as he stared at me over the teapot was intense. He clearly wanted something from me.

"That is true," I said. "Or at least I like to think so."

"Chaz said that was how you felt, but I wasn't sure. Not until this moment."

"You like Chaz," I said bluntly.

"Very much," he admitted softly. "But I'm in a precarious position."

"So is he."

"Of course. I simply mean... I am close to many powerful people. It helps in my line of work. But that would not protect me nor anyone else close to me if anyone uncovered the truth."

"The truth about you preferring men, you mean." I found being blunt often helped things along.

He gave me a long look, then gave a quick nod. So small one might not have noticed if one didn't look closely. That was likely all I was getting from him. Not that I blamed him. He could find himself doing 10 years hard time simply on someone's say so.

"In my experience," I said, shaking the remains of a pillow out of its case, "the very best place to hide is right under people's noses. You wouldn't believe the number of scandalous romance novels I read during my father's fire and brimstone church services."

"Your father is a vicar?" His eyes widened.

"Yes. Very old school. One of those sorts that disapproves of everything. I had to hide everything from lipstick to chewing gum to pin money. The novels were the most difficult to hide. I kept those under the floorboards. Speaking of hiding..." I ducked down under the nightstand and pulled out a thin book with a black leather cover. "Whoever trashed this place may have thought to look under the bed, but they forgot about other pieces of furniture. "I think this is her diary. Maybe between it and her work notebook, we'll uncover a clue. Find anything?"

He lifted the lid on the teapot and peered inside. "Nothing but a few pound notes. Likely her household money. I suppose we'd better call the police now and report the break in."

"Lovely. I so look forward to spending more time with Detective Inspector North."

Chapter 9

While I'd been loath to call in the police, I knew James was right about doing so. Unfortunately, that would mean we'd have to admit to breaking and entering. Well, entering anyway.

"I have an idea," I said as we awaited their arrival. We'd decided we might as well stay in the flat since we could hardly pretend we hadn't been inside. Besides which, it was far more comfortable on Mabel's sofa, once we'd returned the cushions to their proper positions, than standing around in the hall.

James lifted a brow. "Do you?" He didn't sound very excited.

"Yes. I don't want the police knowing we found the key or the notebooks or that we're investigating anything. You know Mr. Evans wants us to be discrete." I also didn't want them asking too many questions and discovering I had Mabel's diary.

"Then what do you want to tell them?" he asked. "We'll need a cover story. They already know you found the body, so you can't pretend you were here to meet her."

"And she doesn't have a roommate." I huffed. "Really, this is most inconvenient."

He chuckled. "I think we're going to have to go with the truth."

Unfortunately, he was right. "I know, we can tell them the thief took the key."

"Why would the thief take the key if he'd already broken in?"

Curses. Foiled again. "I guess if we need to come back, I'll just have to pick the lock."

Before he could respond to that, there was heavy clomping on the stairs. The police were coming.

Naturally North was the assigned detective, and he immediately homed in on me as the most likely person to be guilty of something. Anything. Never mind James was with me and we'd had a key. Although we did not admit to being on the case. Instead, James claimed to be an acquaintance of Mabel's who wanted to return a book he'd borrowed.

"Really." North crossed his arms, the hem of his trench coat riding up. "You decided to return a book you'd borrowed from a dead woman."

"She wasn't dead at the time I borrowed it," James said smoothly. "And I felt that her family might wish to have it."

North's eyes narrowed. "Where is it now?"

James nodded toward a stack of books sitting on one of the side tables. "There. They were on the floor when we arrived. I'm afraid I picked up a bit without thinking. Force of habit." He smiled blandly.

North scowled. "And you got the key from where exactly?"

"Oh, that was me," I said, raising my hand. "It was on Mabel's desk the other night. I picked it up without thinking."

"You're in the habit of doing a lot of things without thinking, aren't you, Lady Rample?" North snarled.

"Hear, hear, old man," James warned.

"And you." North whirled back to James. "Where were you last night when Mabel Pierce was murdered?"

James lifted a brow. "I was out all night."

"Out where?" North gritted.

"I had drinks at my club, followed by the opera and a late supper with friends. I can give you a list if you like. I'm certain they will vouch for my whereabouts."

North's cheeks were ruddy, and his eyes were squintier than ever. Clearly, he did not enjoy his "prime suspects" having ironclad alibis. "Detective Sergeant Plummer."

A slender man of about thirty with pale ginger hair stepped forward. Unlike North, his suit was neatly pressed, his shoes polished to a high sheen, and his trench coat almost new. "Yes, guv?"

"Mr. Woodward here will give you a list of names. I want you to check his alibi with each and every one of them." North's eyes glittered almost meanly.

"Yes, guv." Plummer whipped out a notebook and pencil, eyes trained on James.

"As for you, miss." North turned toward me with some menace.

"It's 'my lady' to you, Detective," I said coolly, inspecting a cuticle.

He literally growled. "*My lady*, then. It would behoove you to stay out of police business."

"It's hardly my fault you keep following me about London. I'd swear you have a little crush on me, Detective."

North turned seventeen shades of red.

DS Plummer pressed a fist to his mouth to keep from laughing out loud.

"It's *Detective Inspector*," North spluttered. "And you do realize I can throw you in jail."

"Not unless I do something illegal. Which I haven't." I stood, gathering my handbag. "I think I shall leave you to it. Coming James?"

"I'll be right with you." There was laughter in his voice.

"As for you, *Detective Inspector,* I shall bid you good day."

He went to step in front of me, and I shot him a glare.

"I said *good day*." And I sailed past him out the door, head held high, nose in the air. My finest lady of the manor impression.

Aunt Butty would be so proud.

I had reached the landing when I heard pounding on the stairs below. Someone else was ascending. Several someones, in fact, by the sounds of it. Surely North hadn't felt the need for more police?

Only it wasn't the police. Men in suits jogged up the stairs, passing me with nary a glance. I'd no doubt they were headed for Mabel's flat, but why? And who were they?

I continued down the stairs at a slower pace, eyeing each man as he passed. There were an awful lot of them simply for a flat that had been broken into. And then came the last man. His portly form was dressed in a suit like the rest, but his was from Saville Row. Gray hair ringed a bald dome and he chomped on a cigar. I recognized him instantly.

"Why, Mr. Pennyfather, whatever are you doing here?" I asked.

Louise's husband glanced up at me from several steps below, his expression a complete blank. I'd never want to play poker with him. Then a smile creased his face, but it felt... fake somehow. As if he'd practiced it in the mirror one time too many.

"Ah, Lady Rample, lovely to see you." He drew abreast of me and bowed over my hand in that elegant way older gentlemen have. I wasn't buying it.

"Are you here on government business?" I teased. It was a known fact that he did something for the government, but nobody was sure what. Some joked he was a spy. Something Louise had always scoffed at. Now I was beginning to wonder, although what the government wanted with Mabel's flat was beyond me.

A muscle ticked in his jaw, but otherwise he gave no indication my words had any effect on him. Instead, he let out a chuckle. Was it me or did it sound forced? "You have quite the imagination, just like your aunt."

"Thank you. I'll take that as a compliment."

"Were you here visiting a friend?" he asked smoothly.

I glanced upward. While this building was decent, it wasn't the sort of place friends of mine generally frequented. "More like acquaintances. Mabel Pierce. But she's unfortunately passed."

"Yes, I'm aware," he said grimly. "You didn't know her well?"

So he *was* here for Mabel. Or her flat anyway. Goodness, I'd have all sorts of juicy gossip for Aunt

Butty. "No, not well at all. We only met the other day at the museum."

He nodded. "Well, I'm sure I'll see you around. I must get to work. Good day, my lady."

"Mr. Pennyfather."

He tipped an imaginary hat and strode purposefully up the steps. I watched until he was out of sight. He never looked back.

How strange.

I continued down, my mind in a whirl. What did Mr. Pennyfather have to do with Mabel Pierce? And why the slew of mysterious men?

This whole business was dashed odd.

Chapter 10

"Hale, darling, what are you doing home?" I asked, leaning over to press a kiss to his cheek.

I'd found him in the sitting room, reading the paper. He looked devilishly handsome in a cream polo shirt and casual tan colored wide leg trousers. A soft, jazzy tune played on the turntable and a cup of coffee steamed on the burlwood end table.

He caught me and slung me over and onto his lap, setting the paper aside. "Band's got the night off tonight. There's a special act at the club."

I looped my arms around his neck. "Well, it'll be nice to see your face for more than five minutes."

He chuckled, then gave me a scorcher of a kiss. It might have gone on longer, but someone cleared his throat.

I jerked back, glancing at the sitting room doorway. "Oh, ah, Hale... You've met James."

Hale nodded at our guest but didn't release me. "Afternoon, James. What were you two up to?"

"A little light breaking and entering," I said breezily. "In fact, I could use a drink." I scrambled off his lap and sauntered over to the drinks cart. "Gentlemen?"

"Scotch and soda, thanks, love," Hale said, polishing off his coffee.

James nodded. "Same for me. In the meantime, may I use your phone to ring my contact?"

"Sure. Out in the hall." While he went to do that, I fixed the men scotch and sodas and a Highball for me. James returned just as I passed them around. "Anything?" I asked him.

"According to my police contact, other than Mabel Pierce's coat and handbag, which they took for evidence, they found nothing of interest in her office."

"So they didn't take any files?"

"Apparently not." He took a long swallow of his scotch and soda. "Also, they did not arrive at the flat until after we did, and then were kicked out of it shortly thereafter. So nothing there either."

That settled that question. "We'll definitely need to speak to Evans about the missing file, then."

"Agreed."

"Why would Louise's husband be at Mabel's flat, do you think?" I mused.

"Louise?" James asked.

"Louise Pennyfather. Her husband does something with the government. I've never known what—I'm not sure anyone does, not even Louise. But he was there today, and he had a bunch of men in suits with him."

"Cops?" Hale's forehead creased. He wasn't a fan, seeing as how they'd once arrested him for murder. He'd been totally innocent, of course. Fortunately, I'd been able to prove it.

I shook my head. "No. But maybe something like cops."

"Government agents," James said grimly. "I was still in the flat when they arrived and threw North and his men out. Said they were taking over the investigation."

My eyes widened. "Government agents don't investigate murder. Did they say who they were?"

James shook his head. "At least not that I could hear, though they flashed a badge at North. That's what got him moving. Otherwise, he wasn't about to comply. I can only imagine that whoever they are, they outrank North by a lot."

"They'd have to," I murmured. "That man doesn't comply with anyone."

"G-Men," Hale said over the rim of his glass.

I stared at him a beat. "What?"

"Government men," he said. "That's what we call the FBI—the Federal Bureau of Investigation—back home. Sounds a bit like the men that were with this Pennyfather guy. You got anything like that here?"

"MI5," James said grimly. "And Ophelia is right. They don't investigate murder."

"What would MI5 want with Mabel's flat?" I protested. "She worked at a museum, for goodness' sake."

James shrugged. "Doesn't mean anything. Working at a museum is perfect undercover work for a criminal or a spy. Easy enough to smuggle things in and out of the country along with the artifacts. Stolen goods, drugs, information."

"Please." I pshawed. "Mabel Pierce did not strike me as the sort of person to play at spy craft."

"Which is why she'd be a perfect spy," Hale pointed out. "Look at Mata Hari. Who would suspect a dancer?"

He had a point. Still, I had a hard time believing Mabel was anything other than she'd presented herself to be. She'd seemed so... well, perhaps nice wasn't the word, but so focused on her career, so ordinary. And why would MI5 search her flat and not the museum where, presumably, the secrets or whatnot would be smuggled out of the country? No, it simply didn't make sense unless, of course, they thought she was hiding something important in her flat.

In any case, they hadn't got her diary or the notebook from her office. I did. I opened my handbag and pulled them out. "Maybe there are some answers here."

"How did you manage to smuggle that out?" James asked.

It was my turn to shrug. "It wasn't hard. I simply tucked it away on my person. Other than North taking a quick look in my bag, nobody ever bothered to search me. Once I was out of the flat, I put it in my bag. Figured he wouldn't search there twice."

"Clever girl," Hale said approvingly. "What's the diary say?"

I flipped through to the last entry, the day before she was murdered. "How very dull. She merely talks about her day at work, what she had for lunch, complains about Mr. Evans. No shock there. They clearly didn't get along."

"Go further back," James suggested. "The goddess statue was taken before that."

I nodded and turned to the day of the theft. "There isn't much. She says, 'Another artifact stolen today. Beginning to think something is very wrong at this museum. Keeping a close eye on X.' Who is X, I wonder?"

"I don't recall anyone with a name beginning with X," James said.

"I'm assuming it's a place holder," I pointed out. "Sort of a code. Just in case someone gets their hands on the diary. Although why she'd be worried about that in her flat is beyond me."

"Unless she really is a spy," Hale reminded me.

I remembered that both Foster and Prentiss had mentioned visiting Mabel to see the statue two days before it was stolen, so I turned to that page and read aloud. "'Both Prentiss and Foster stopped by to see the statue today. Foster's an old blowhard. Why he gets all the funding is beyond me. Prentiss is alright, though I don't know why a dinosaur guy wants to poke his nose into my work.' She goes on to talk about what she had for lunch and how annoying Evans was."

"No mention of Mr. X," James mused. "I guess we can rule out those three men since she calls them by name."

I shook my head. "I disagree. She only uses the moniker 'Mr. X' when there's sensitive information involved. Visits from Prentiss and Foster or arguments with Evans are hardly anything she needs to hide. Suspicions about whoever Mr. X is certainly are."

"Fair point. What about the other thefts?" James prompted. "Is there anything in there about those?"

"Unfortunately, I have no idea when those thefts happened," I said, flipping through the pages, trying to see if anything popped out at me. "I'm afraid I'll have to spend a little time reading more thoroughly."

"Well, I'll leave you to it then," James said, draining his glass.

"I'll have Maddie show you out— Oh, wait. She's out with Simon." Simon was Aunt Butty's chauffeur. The two of them had been seeing each other for several months now, and it wasn't uncommon for them to meet up in the afternoons when Aunt Butty didn't need a driver.

"No need," James assured me. "I know the way."

We made our adieus, and James exited the sitting room. His footsteps echoed across the marble floor in the entry, then the door opened and shut. Hale opened his mouth to speak, but I placed a finger over my lips. Although we'd agreed to work together and share information, I didn't totally trust James. I don't mean to say I thought he was involved in anything nefarious, just that I couldn't count on him not investigating behind my back.

I got up and tiptoed to the doorway, craning my neck to get a good look without anyone—

hopefully—seeing me. "Coast is clear." I breathed a sigh of relief and turned around.

Hale raised a brow. "Clear for what?"

"My plan."

"I thought you agreed to work with Woodward."

"I did, and I'll share anything of importance I learn, but I have contacts he doesn't."

"Ah, Mrs. Pennyfather."

"Exactly. I'm going to ring her up and ask her to set up a meeting with her husband."

His other brow went up. "If he really is with MI5, are you sure that's wise?"

"Of course I am." I definitely wasn't. "I have a feeling there's more going on than simply a missing artifact, and I want to know what that is and how Mabel was involved."

He sighed. "At least I have the night off so I can go with you."

"I don't know that she'll be able to set up something so quickly, but don't worry. If you can't come, I'll take Chaz."

I did not, in fact, take Chaz. It wasn't my fault. Louise had set up the appointment with her husband late the following afternoon. Chaz had a prior engagement and couldn't come. Hale had already left for the club. I could have asked James, but I felt I could get more information out of Mr. Pennyfather if it was just me. After all, I could call upon my feminine wiles when needed.

"What time will you be home, m'lady?" Maddie asked as she helped me shrug on my new spring green swing jacket. "I only ask because I don't want your supper getting cold."

"You're not cooking, are you?" I asked, aghast. Since Maddie wasn't much of a cook, I often dined out or ate with my Aunt Butty. Simple meals were thrown together from Fortnum and Mason hampers or trips to Harrods' Food Hall or the occasional time when Aunt Butty's cook—who everyone simply referred to as "Cook"—took pity on me and sent me home with mounds of food.

"Of course not." Maddie tutted. "You ought to know better. I don't have the time to muck about in the kitchen. Your aunt's cook made some meals for you. Says you don't eat enough." She snorted as she gave my voluptuous figure a once over.

"Don't make me fire you," I warned.

She snorted again. "As if."

"Very well," I huffed. "I can't imagine this will take long. I should be home within a couple of hours."

I hurried down the steps and into my car, which purred to life when I started it up. Marvelous invention, the automobile.

Horns honked and tires squealed as I pulled out onto the street with barely a glance. Really, people ought to watch more closely. It was a lovely afternoon, and I enjoyed the brief drive to the address in Mayfair Louise had given me. Only when I reached the street, it was blocked off for some sort of road works. The address I needed was on the other side of the block. I could park here and walk or pull down the side street and around the block. Less walking that way. Around the block it was!

Turning right, I drove carefully down the narrow street when an elderly man stepped right in front of me. I slammed on the brakes, my heart thumping wildly in my chest. I waved at him to carry on, but he stood there in the middle of the road, staring at me from beneath his battered fedora like a country bumpkin.

Finally, I rolled down the window and stuck my head out. "Hullo! Do be a darling and move out of my way, please. I'm in a bit of a hurry."

He stared some more. Was he hard of hearing?

I heaved a sigh. "I say, is everything alright?"

Nothing. Just a blank stare. It was odd though. I'd thought him to be an old man based upon the bushy gray hair sprouting from beneath his hat and the matching mustache and beard that went halfway down his chest, but his skin was remarkably unlined.

I was about to open my mouth when something hard and cold pressed against the back of my head and a grim male voice said, "I have a gun. Don't make a sound."

I froze. Highwaymen in the middle of London seemed a bit out of place.

"Nod if you understand."

I nodded. What else was there to do?

The door opened, and the car shifted as the gunman climbed in the back seat. My gaze slid toward the rearview mirror, but he barked, "Don't look in the mirror."

Now I wanted to look more than anything. Still, I managed to keep my eyes straight ahead.

He must have beckoned because the elderly bumpkin shoved his hands in his pockets and stepped aside. A sly smile curved his lips beneath his mustache and beard. He was obviously in on this, whatever this was.

"Now drive," the gunman said.

I put my hands on the wheel. "Drive where?"

"Just do it," he snarled. "And don't try anything funny."

I had no idea what sort of funny thing he thought I'd do with a gun to my head. I pressed the gas and started forward, pulling to a stop at the stop sign at the end of the block.

"Turn right."

That led me away from where I was supposed to meet Mr. Pennyfather. Still, there was nothing for it. I turned right.

For the next few minutes, we drove through the streets of London into a rather dodgy part of Soho. I wasn't sure if we were going the most direct route to wherever he was taking me, or if he was trying to confuse me. Unlucky for him, I'd an excellent mind for directions. Unlucky for me, he never once removed the gun from the back of my skull. I was almost getting used to it.

At last, he said, "Park here."

The car lurched a bit as I stamped on the brake in front of a derelict brick building of dubious nature. Fortunately, he didn't shoot me.

"Get out."

As I climbed out of the car, I realized we were still in Soho, but not terribly far from the museum. Was this related somehow? It must be, though how I couldn't fathom. I started to turn, but the gun was suddenly pressed into my lower back.

"Not so fast." He tutted, grabbing one arm in a vise grip, and pressing the gun harder into my back. "Now move." He prodded me toward the building with its grimy windows and peeling door.

I knew without a shadow of a doubt that if I went inside that building, the chances of me coming out again were slim to none. No, I was not going to go along meekly. But what could I do without any weapons?

A slow smile crept across my face. I did have a weapon. One a brute like him would never see coming.

"Oh, dear," I said. "I feel faint."

"What—?"

I let my knees buckle and my upper body sag, the sudden movement loosening his grip on my arm. The pressure of the gun eased from my back as the man panicked over a fainting woman.

Without a moment's thought, I slung my handbag out, whacking the gun from his hand. It hit the ground and clattered away, sliding out of sight under a pile of rubbish. My nights dancing with Chaz at the jazz clubs came in handy as I whirled on the ball of one foot, ripping my arm free. One knee came up and found its mark. The man doubled over with a howl, clutching his family jewels, and I whacked him on the back of the head with my handbag, then took off running.

I didn't know how long it would take the man to recover, find his gun, and come after me, so I didn't dawdle. I ran pell-mell down the street, turning the corner quickly and dashing down another narrow backstreet until it spilled onto a main road.

Across the street was a pub. Perfect. I darted across and made my way inside. The air was thick and blue with smoke and stank of old cigarettes and beer. Peeling posters advertising prize fights papered the walls, and the windows looked like they hadn't been washed in a century. Heads turned and eyes widened. Ladies didn't exactly frequent pubs, particularly aristocratic ladies. I gave everyone an airy smile and a nod as I made my way to the bar.

"We don't serve ladies in here," the barkeep snarled. He was a thick man—thick in shoulder, waist, and arm—with layers of fat over muscle. His sleeves were rolled up, a tattoo of a pugilist on one forearm. He glared at me through small, brown eyes set a little too close together.

"I am not here for a drink," I assured him. "I need to use your telephone. It's an emergency."

He stared at me. "It's for customers only."

I sighed. "I will pay for the trouble." I dug in my purse, pulled out a few coins, and slapped them on the bar.

His eyes widened at what was no doubt a ridiculous amount and thrust a finger at a phone booth in the corner. "Over there. Help yourself."

"Thank you, darling," I said, and eased my way past rickety tables and staring eyes to the phone booth. I quickly dialed my aunt's number. Mr. Singh picked up on the third ring. "Mr. Singh, I have a bit of a dilemma."

Shéa MacLeod

Chapter 11

While he refused to sell me any liquor, the barman did finally offer me an overly sweetened cup of tea once I pulled out my best lady of the manor impression along with a great deal of fluttering in my damsel-in-distress role. I wasn't above using such things if they got me what I wanted. More or less. It's a man's world, and a woman must use every tool at her disposal.

I found myself a seat with a good view of the entry and the grimy window facing the street so I could watch for anyone following me. So far, so good—if I ignored the stares from the other clientele.

I imagined they didn't get too many females in this establishment, and they weren't thrilled about having one now.

As I sipped my sickly-sweet beverage, I mulled over recent events. I was now sure that the supposed elderly man was, in fact, not elderly at all but in a disguise. Unfortunately, I wasn't sure I'd recognize him again without said disguise. The gunman, on the other hand, had stood out. I'd caught a glimpse of his face when I'd kneed him. He'd had pockmarked skin along his jaw and a small scar through his upper lip as if it had been cut in a fight and never properly healed. Him I would definitely recognize if I saw him again.

A good thirty minutes later, Mr. Singh finally arrived, pushing through the door, and filling the space with his unflappable elegance. He was subjected to even more intense stares than I'd been, but he ignored them, pacing toward my table through the clouds of smoke. He gave a slight bow. "My lady. This is becoming a bad habit."

"You're not wrong there." This wasn't the first time he'd had to rescue me from a sticky situation. I drained the last of my tea and stood, touching my cloche hat to make sure it was secure. "I'm getting rather tired of being chased about the city and kidnapped willy-nilly. Simon's with you?"

He nodded. "In the car. This way." He held out his arm, indicating I should go first.

We made it to the sidewalk without incident, and I breathed a sigh of relief at the comparably fresh air. I still felt as if I was being stared at through the window, but I chalked that down to nerves. Or perhaps they were staring, but so be it. I had better things to focus my attention on.

Aunt Butty's Bentley pulled to the curb, the engine purring like a very large kitten, and Mr. Singh opened the back door so I could climb in. Once I was seated, he hopped up front with Simon.

"'Lo, m'lady," Simon said cheerily. "Heard you got yourself in a spot of bother."

"That's putting it mildly, Simon."

"Glad you're in one piece. If you'll point me in the direction of your car?" My kidnapping apparently barely registered on his list of Bizarre Things That Happen. After all, he worked for Aunt Butty.

I gave him directions and he steered the large car through traffic and up and down narrow side streets with ease, finally pulling up behind my car which was still parked exactly where I'd left it.

He stared up at the building. "Bit dodgy, innit?"

"Indeed. Fortunately, I never made it inside." I started to clamber from the car, but Mr. Singh held up a hand.

"If my lady doesn't mind, I will drive her car and Simon will follow. If those ruffians are still about, I don't want them getting their hands on you."

Fair point. I nodded. "Thank you, Mr. Singh."

We watched as Mr. Singh climbed into my car and the engine purred to life. He pulled out, driving at a sedate pace. We carefully followed along behind him as he wended his way to my townhouse.

"You still don't know why they took you?" Simon asked, eyes on the road and my cobalt blue vehicle.

"Unfortunately, no. And I never got to finish my errand." I didn't mention who I had been going to meet. Not that I was worried about Simon's discretion—he'd been helpful in a number of investigations. It was more that I didn't want to mention Mr. Pennyfather's involvement until I knew precisely what that involvement was.

"That's too bad," he tutted. "Perhaps you can reschedule."

"Perhaps." I'd have to give Louise a ring. Hopefully her husband wouldn't be too upset I hadn't shown and would still be willing to see me. Only this time, I'd take Chaz with me as a deterrent to any possible kidnappers. Harder to snatch two people than one.

When we finally arrived back at my house, Mr. Singh went to park my car while Simon ushered me to the door. He waited on the doorstep as I unlocked the front door. I could have rung and waited for Maddie, but it seemed ridiculous to interrupt her when I had a key.

"Do you want to come inside for a cup of tea and some biscuits?" I asked. "I'm sure Maddie would love to see you."

He grinned. "Thanks, m'lady. Awful kind. But no. I got to get back, as does Mr. Singh. And I've got a date with Maddie tomorrow."

"Wonderful." I gave him a warm smile. "You've been good for her, you know."

Slight pink tinged his cheeks. "Nice of you to say, but it's her that's good for me."

"Let's say you're good for each other and leave it at that." I pushed open the door. "Thank you, Simon, for coming to my rescue. And thank Mr. Singh for me, too."

"Sure thing, m'lady." He doffed his cap then turned and hurried down the steps and back to the Bentley where Mr. Singh now stood.

They both waited until I shut the door. Only once I had did I hear the powerful motor rev as the car pulled away. I let out a sigh of relief. It was good to be home.

I headed straight to the telephone and rang Louise. She picked up immediately.

"Why, Ophelia, I thought you'd be with Mr. Pennyfather," she said in her loud, braying voice.

"I was unavoidably detained," I said dryly. "On my way to see him, I was waylaid by ruffians who tried to kidnap me."

"Good heavens! That's dreadful. Are you alright, my dear girl?"

"Yes. Yes. I'm fine, but I'll need to reschedule with Mr. Pennyfather if you can manage."

"But of course. Once he arrives home, I'll have a word. Ring you as soon as I do." After a few more pleasantries, she hung up.

After shucking off my lightweight coat, gloves, and hat, I hung them over the banister and made my way into the sitting room where I rang for Maddie. While I waited, I fixed myself a whiskey straight up. Sometimes life just called for unadulterated alcohol.

"M'lady, you're home early," Maddie said as she bustled into the room. "Tea?"

"Yes, please. And make it strong. And biscuits. Cake, too, if you've got it. Probably some sandwiches. Yes, a sandwich would do nicely. But don't forget to put lots of butter on it." The last thing anyone needed was a dry sandwich.

"So basically, a full afternoon tea then," she said dryly.

I shrugged. "Call it what you will, but I need sustenance."

"It'll ruin your supper."

"So be it."

"Should I make some for Mr. Hale, too?"

"I thought he was at the club." He'd left before I had.

"He was. They were practicing a new tune but took a break until later tonight. He played it for me on the piano." She looked like she'd sucked a lemon.

"Not to your taste?"

"Hardly. Sounded like a lot of caterwauling to me."

I repressed a smile. "Well, then, you go ready the tea. I'll see if he wants to come down."

"No need. I'm here." Hale sauntered into the room, already dressed for the jazz club in his tuxedo. "And tea is just the ticket. Thanks, Maddie." His tone turned teasing. "Even if you do find my music to be mere 'caterwauling.'"

Maddie turned red as a tomato. She opened and shut her mouth a few times, as if trying to come up with something to say, before finally blurting, "Sure thing, Mr. Hale." She bustled out, cheeks blazing.

"Why do you tease her so?" I asked with an amused sigh.

"Because she begs for it," he said with a laugh.

"Whiskey?" I asked, holding up the tumbler which I hadn't yet drunk from. He took it from me while I poured myself another glass. "What time do you have to leave?"

"About an hour." He eyed me. "You look a bit flustered."

"I feel a bit flustered," I admitted, though I'd admit it to no one but him. And possibly Chaz. Or my friend Phil, if she was around, but since she was up in Yorkshire at the moment, I'd have to catch her up later. "I had a spot of kidnapping this afternoon."

He raised a brow. "Were you the kidnapper or the kidnappee?"

"Kidnappee," I assured him. "Although I love that you think I have the skills to be a kidnapper."

"You can do anything you set your mind to, love. That I know." He leaned down and pressed a kiss to my temple before taking a seat in one of the cozy chairs next to the window overlooking the garden. "Now, tell me about this kidnapping."

"Attempted kidnapping," I corrected him. I told him about going to meet with Mr. Pennyfather and how I'd been held at gunpoint and forced to drive to a dodgy part of town. "Fortunately, I was able to get away and call Mr. Singh. He and Simon came to my rescue."

"Good old Mr. Singh. Can always count on him for a clean getaway," Hale teased. Then he gave me an appraising look. "Were the kidnappers after you specifically, or just in a general highway robbing mood?"

I mulled it over. "Me specifically, I believe. They certainly seemed to know who I was, and I'm certain there were other cars and drivers about they could have held up if they were simply after money."

His expression turned grim. "You know what that means."

I shrugged. "I suppose it means they knew where I was to be and when."

"Exactly. And who knew that you would be in that part of town at that precise time?"

I frowned. "You did. Or rather, you knew I was meeting Mr. Pennyfather and generally when, but not where. Same with Maddie."

"So who did know?" he prodded.

"Only Louise and Mr. Pennyfather," I said. "She's the one that set it up and of course he would know since he's the one I was meeting. But Louise would never try and kidnap me. She'd have no reason to."

"Which leaves precisely one person," he agreed.

My eyes widened. "Surely Mr. Pennyfather wouldn't have had me kidnapped," I protested.

"He was the only other person who knew where you'd be and when, so he was the only one who could have passed that information to the kidnappers."

It made sense, sort of. "But why?"

"That you'll have to ask him."

And I would. Once Louise set up another meeting. Yes, this time I would definitely take Chaz. And maybe a gun.

Shéa MacLeod

Chapter 12

The next day, James rang and asked me to meet him at the museum. I agreed at once. It would give me a good opportunity to tell him what had happened.

It was a drizzly day, so I grabbed an umbrella on my way out the door. Fortunately, it wasn't coming down too hard, so I should stay dry enough.

Once I parked, I dodged puddles on my way to the entrance, then edged my way carefully up the wide, shallow marble steps which would no doubt be slick from the rain. A herd of school children shrieked with laughter as they dashed around the courtyard in front of the museum, splashing in puddles and climbing bronze statues of British kings while their teacher shouted in annoyance.

Patrons milled about the museum entry hall, voices echoing off the high ceiling, shrugging into or out of coats while attendants carefully tucked away dripping umbrellas behind the coat check. A lone cleaner swiped at the floor with a dry mop in an unending quest to keep the floor from becoming a veritable danger zone.

After handing over my own coat and umbrella—and receiving a claim ticket which I tucked in my handbag—I walked through the rotunda and took the main flight of stairs to the next floor and the Special Collections Room where James had told me to meet him. I caught sight of him immediately, as the room was empty save for him and a blond haired man standing in front of a jewelry display with his back to me.

"James." I strode toward him, my heels tapping against the floor.

He turned with a smile. "Ophelia. I have had an idea."

"What is it?"

"I believe I know how the goddess statue was stolen."

"Go on," I urged.

"We already know that there was a maintenance placard placed on the door to prevent anyone entering."

I nodded.

"I believe what we're looking at here is at least two thieves. The first thief enters the museum as an ordinary visitor, puts the maintenance placard on the door and shuts it behind him, then removes the statue from its display and wraps it to prevent damage." He mimed each of the actions.

"With you so far," I agreed.

"Next, the thief exits the room, closing the door behind him and leaving the placard in place to prevent immediate discovery of the theft." He strode across the room and out the door with me hot on his trail. "He walks to the end of the hall here and the emergency exit." He paused in front of the window, lifting the sash.

"Right, but the ladder wasn't touched," I pointed out.

"That's because Thief One didn't leave the museum by the emergency exit. Instead, he tossed the statue out the window down to where Thief Two was waiting."

I clapped my hands. "That's brilliant. Then Thief One shuts the window and walks out of the museum, no one the wiser."

"That or he simply went back to work."

"That would make sense. It's unlikely the guards would have noticed one of the employees walking around," I agreed.

"In any case, they pulled it off rather brilliantly. Although I'm not certain it leads us any closer to the truth, other than the fact there *could* have been an inside man but didn't necessarily need to be, at least not in the actual theft. I'm still convinced that at the very least someone was passing along information to the thieves."

"I agree with you there. Doesn't make sense otherwise," I said, taking his arm as we strolled back down the hall and headed for the stairs back to the rotunda. "By the by, I think there's something else you should know."

"What's that?"

"I was somewhat kidnapped yesterday."

He stopped abruptly. "How can a person be somewhat kidnapped?"

"Well, I was on my way to see Mr. Pennyfather about what happened at Mabel's flat. I was about to park when a ruffian jumped in the car and put a gun to my head. Forced me to drive to someplace in SoHo."

"And you got away? Without being shot?" He sounded incredulous.

"Well, yes. I have a few tricks up my sleeve. Once I was free, I made my way to the nearest pub and rang Mr. Singh."

"Mr. Singh?"

"My aunt's butler."

"That clears things up," he said dryly.

"Mr. Singh was in the Indian Army during the Great War," I explained. "He has... interesting skills. He's helped me out of a number of scrapes. In any case, I am fine now, but I still don't know who these men were or why they'd want to kidnap me."

"I imagine it's related to the case somehow," he said.

"Naturally. But why me and not you?"

He frowned. "Could it have something to do with whatever Mr. Pennyfather is up to and your visit with him?"

"Could do," I agreed. "But it's hard to say as we've no idea what that is."

"What did these men look like?" he asked as we slowly descended the steps.

"I've never seen either of them before in my life. Unfortunately, the man who stepped in front of my car was wearing a gray wig and fake mustache and beard. I'm not entirely sure I would recognize him. I only caught a brief glimpse of the gunman. He had a scar on his face and pockmarked cheeks."

"You mean like that man?" James asked quietly, nodding toward four men huddled at the bottom of the steps, off to the side.

I glanced to where he pointed, and my jaw nearly hit the floor.

For there, chatting to Mr. Evans and Mr. Pennyfather, were two men in plain suits. One of them was the blond man I'd seen upstairs and one of them was the pockmarked gunman who'd kidnapped me.

"What's he doing here?" I hissed, shooting daggers at Mr. Pennyfather from behind the large column where we'd taken refuge. "And with those men! Is Mr. Evans in on it, do you think?"

"Your guess is as good as mine. But I will say I am doubly sure this has something to do with the missing goddess statue."

"And Mabel's death," I reminded him.

"Yes, of course. I'm certain, as you are, the two things are related. I just don't see as yet how."

"We should follow Mr. Pennyfather when he leaves."

James shook his head. "If Mr. Pennyfather is with MI5 as we suspect, he will no doubt be surrounded by agents who won't be particularly pleased to see us. Look how your last attempt went. No, we should question Mr. Evans. He's obviously in this up to his eyeballs."

He had a point. Still, Mr. Evans would no doubt be here later. Mr. Pennyfather, on the other hand, had a bad habit of leaving the country for weeks at a time and with no advanced warning. If he left now, we'd never get the chance to talk to him. I didn't want to miss out on the opportunity. But I also didn't want James to try and prevent me from it.

I smiled blandly. "Of course. Great idea."

He nodded. "I thought so. Look. They're leaving."

Sure enough, Mr. Pennyfather turned and strode toward the front door while the two kidnappers headed to the back. I wouldn't mind talking to them either, but clearly, they were minor fish compared to Mr. Pennyfather. I'd bet he knew exactly what they'd been up to. Maybe even been behind it. Although I couldn't fathom why he'd want to have me kidnapped.

"Mr. Evans is headed back to his office. Let's go." James left the dubious safety of our column and headed down the stairs. I followed, but only because I needed to get downstairs anyway if I was going to follow Mr. Pennyfather.

When we reached the ground floor, we turned right, and I paused outside the ladies' room. "You go ahead. I need to... freshen up."

James nodded and continued on his way, following Mr. Evans. Poor deluded man. James not Mr. Evans. If he honestly thought I would follow along like a meek little woman, he didn't know me at all.

I let the ladies' room door bang shut behind me, waited a beat, then opened it a crack, watching James stride out of sight. With a smile, I opened it all the way and slipped out, hurrying toward the rotunda and then into the entry hall. It was still raining, but the line to retrieve coats and umbrellas was long. I didn't have time to wait.

Leaving my belongings behind for the moment, I dashed outside just in time to see Mr. Pennyfather exit through the massive wrought iron gates and climb into a car. Dash it all! I needed to get to my vehicle immediately so I could follow.

I was about to run down the stairs when hands grabbed me viciously and dragged me across the steps and into a corner out of sight of museum patrons. I opened my mouth to scream, but a hand was clapped over it. Between that and the rain which had started pouring in earnest, no one would ever hear me.

"Listen, girlie," the rough voice behind me said, "you need to back off. You don't, and it won't go well for you. You'll end up draped over a coffin like your friend."

Mabel! He meant Mabel!

Before I could do any more than realize the truth, he thrust me forward hard. I stumbled and fell to my knees. By the time I righted myself, my accoster was gone, but I knew one thing for sure: I'd just been threatened by one of my would-be kidnappers.

Chapter 13

"What the deuce happened to you?" James stared at my no-doubt disheveled appearance as I met him outside Mr. Evans' door.

"Slipped on the floor. Marble and water, not a good combination." I shrugged and tried to look innocent.

He frowned. I'm not sure he believed me. I decided a change of subject was in order.

"What did you find out?"

"Not much," he admitted. "He claims Mr. Pennyfather is simply a board member who had stopped in to discuss some museum business."

"Sure," I scoffed. "And his muscle?"

James' lips twitched, in amusement probably. "Claimed they were workmen here to fix some broken tiles or some such."

"Likely story. Although they certainly could stand to do something about the slipperiness." I wasn't about to tell him about my run-in. He'd just ask uncomfortable questions. No, I was sticking with my lie. "Did you happen to ask about the files on the stolen items?"

"I did," he said. "Evans claims he has no idea where those files are. They were strictly Mabel's domain, and he never touched them."

"So if he doesn't have them and the police don't have them and they're not in Mabel's office or home, then that means the killer likely took them. Find them, find the murderer."

"Doesn't help much at the moment," he pointed out.

"We're tying the threads together, and eventually we'll have a better picture," I assured him.

We bid each other adieu, I collected my brolly and coat from the check-in, and I climbed in my car. Then I drove straight to Aunt Butty's.

"Good heavens, Ophelia, you look like a drowned rat," she said when Mr. Singh ushered me into her sitting room overlooking Hyde Park.

"That's hardly the case, Aunt Butty. I'm mostly dry if a bit windblown. And I could use a drink." I shot her a look.

"Mr. Singh has already gone to collect tea. Sit down." She waved me toward the settee that had probably been in the family since the Victorian age. "Tell me what's happening."

I caught her up on the investigation, up to and including my near kidnapping followed by the warning issued by the selfsame kidnappers. I finished with, "I really need to have a chat with Mr. Pennyfather. I think he's up to something."

Her eyes widened with excitement. "Really? I'd have never thought it of him. He always seems so mild-mannered. Do you suppose he's up to something nefarious?

I could hardly fathom the portly Mr. Pennyfather doing anything nefarious, but then I'd never suspected he was involved with MI5 either. "I doubt it. Still, something curious is going on."

"So exciting! This could go in my spy novel."

"You're writing a spy novel now?" Last I'd heard, she was working on a gothic romance.

"But of course. Didn't I say? I thought it would be marvelous, good fun. Female spy, naturally." She stood abruptly. "Let me ring Louise and have her pop 'round. I'm sure we can put our heads together and come up with a plan!"

She bustled out of the room, intent on her task, so I helped myself to a brandy from the drinks cupboard. I wasn't a particular fan of brandy, being more of a whiskey and gin person, but Aunt Butty always kept a stock of extremely good cherry brandy, declaring it was excellent for the digestion. I didn't know if that was true or not, but it was delicious, so I didn't much care either way.

Aunt Butty returned, with Mr. Singh close behind carrying a large silver tray which he placed with great aplomb on what my aunt insisted on referring to as the tea table. I quickly polished off my brandy before Aunt Butty could chide me for spoiling my tea or some such.

"Won't you pour, Mr. Singh?" she requested as she piled a small plate with Cook's homemade gingernut biscuits. "I'm famished. I really must fortify myself."

Mr. Singh and I exchanged an amused glance as he poured a cup of tea, dropped two lumps of sugar in it, and handed it to me. I thanked him and took a long sip. What it could really use was a shot of whiskey.

"Did you reach Louise?" I asked, reaching for a gingernut.

"I did. She's on her way. Chaz too."

"Really?" I asked.

She shot Mr. Singh a look. "He made me do it."

Mr. Singh was possibly the only person on the planet who could make Aunt Butty do anything. "I'm impressed."

"The word 'kidnapping' was mentioned," he said dryly. "I thought perhaps young Mr. Raynott should be involved. If for nothing but muscle."

"You told Louise about my kidnapping over the phone?" I asked my aunt, aghast.

"Heavens, no," she said, polishing off a biscuit. "I told her we ought to kidnap her husband."

"I can't believe I let you talk me into this," Chaz muttered as we waited in the stairwell outside Mr. Philpott's office.

"Sure you can," I said.

"You're right. I can." He sighed. "What am I going to tell James?"

"Nothing." I shot him a glare. "You don't tell Woodward a thing, do you hear me? And why would you be talking to him about this anyway? It's not his business."

"Well, it sort of is. The museum board hired him, you know."

My glare grew in intensity.

"Fine. Fine." He held up his hands. "It's not his business in any way, shape, or form."

"And don't you forget it."

Fortunately, before the argument could devolve further, the door swung open and Aunt

Butty popped her head in the stairwell and hissed, "It's a go!"

"She's been watching American detective flicks again, hasn't she?" Chaz moaned.

"Always. Stop your moaning and come on." I grabbed his hand and half dragged him into the hall where Louise's braying voice could easily be heard. The woman didn't even need a megaphone.

"I'm telling you, Mortimer, I won't have it."

Chaz and I exchanged glances. He mouthed, *"Mortimer?"* I shrugged. I'd known the man for years——well, I'd known *of* him——and this was the first I'd heard his given name.

"Now, Louise, it's not what it looks like." Mr. Pennyfather's voice was softer and more placating. Not at all the stern, in-control man I'd met at Mabel's. I couldn't help but be curious about what "it" was and what exactly "it" looked like.

"It looks like you're gambling again," she bellowed.

Ah. That's what it was.

"I assure you I am not." Mr. Pennyfather's voice went up a notch just as Aunt Butty barreled through the door, Chaz and I hot on her heels.

Mr. Pennyfather sat in a leather chair behind a large desk while Louise loomed over him, oozing ire. Peaches had taken up residence on one of the visitor chairs and seemed completely unperturbed by the row. Which was interesting because I'd never taken

Louise to be the rowing sort. She typically did what she wanted to do precisely when she wanted to do it without care for anyone's input. Rather like Aunt Butty. No wonder they got along.

Mr. Pennyfather glared at us. "What is the meaning of this?"

"Oh, stop your complaining, Mortimer, and start explaining," Louise said imperiously.

"That's right. We're concerned," Aunt Butty said, stepping up beside Louise, drawing Mortimer Pennyfather's attention.

"This is none of your concern, Butty," Mr. Pennyfather snapped.

"Don't speak to my dearest friend in that tone of voice!" Louise snapped back.

While they kept "our mark" busy (as Aunt Butty had taken to calling Mr. Pennyfather), Chaz sidled around the other side of the desk, coming up behind him. I stayed more or less in his line of sight, so he'd be distracted. Even a person who worked for MI5 couldn't keep his gaze on four places at once.

"I will speak to her however I like in my own office!" Mr. Pennyfather bellowed, his face turning beet red, clearly at the end of his tether.

At that precise moment, Chaz grabbed Mr. Pennyfather's arms from behind while Aunt Butty whipped a large silk handkerchief from her bosom.

Mr. Pennyfather opened his mouth and bellowed, "What is the meaning of—"

Aunt Butty shoved the handkerchief inside.

"Really, Mortimer, I find your attitude incredibly tiresome," Louise brayed, keeping up the pretense of their conversation. No doubt so that any listening ears wouldn't realize what was really happening.

While she prattled on, Aunt Butty used a second handkerchief to secure the first one in place, muffling his protests. I hurried over to help Chaz truss up Mr. Pennyfather like a Christmas goose.

"Dash it, Louise," Chaz barked, trying to mimic Mr. Pennyfather's voice with only moderate success. A mimic he was not.

"Don't you speak that way to me either," Louise all but bellowed. Her eyes sparkled. She was clearly enjoying this.

With Mr. Pennyfather securely tied and gagged and no one the wiser, Louise scooped up Peaches and Chaz frog-marched "our mark" to the door. I opened it, sticking my head out far enough to make sure the coast was clear before beckoning everyone out.

Louise paused in the open doorway and managed one last, "I've had quite enough of this, Mortimer. I'm going home. Good day!" And she slammed the office door behind her.

We must have looked like a mad circus, trooping down the hall and into the stairwell, but we managed it. Surprisingly, no one came to check on the loud argument—no doubt not wanting to get involved and being equal parts embarrassed and thrilled they'd had to overhear the drama—and we got away free. Once downstairs, I went to get my car and pulled right up so they could hustle Mr. Pennyfather in without anyone noticing we were dragging around a kidnap victim.

The irony was not lost on me.

Still, needs must, and Mr. Pennyfather had some explaining to do.

Shéa MacLeod

Chapter 14

Prior to our foray into kidnapping, we had discussed the pros and cons of storing our victim at various locations. Chaz didn't have the space and the Pennyfathers' servants would likely notice something amiss, so it had been a tossup between Aunt Butty's place or mine. I'd won the coin toss—so to speak— since I lived in a townhouse, and she lived three floors up. Much easier to get him into my home unnoticed.

To that end, Mr. Pennyfather was currently trussed up in my sitting room while Chaz made himself useful mixing cocktails. Maddie had thrust a half empty bottle of wine at him and told him he better make use of it, or she would. I had no idea why we had a half-used bottle of wine—not being in the habit of leaving such things undrunk—and I was afraid to ask. Chaz was thrilled and was mixing up something involving red wine and rum which he called The Bishop. It sounded atrocious, but I was game for anything.

"I had one at the Waldorf-Astoria in New York," he said, giving the cocktail shaker a vigorous shake. "Marvelous. It'll put hair on your chest, as the Americans say."

"Dear boy," Louise said dryly, "no one here but you wants excess hair on their person."

He chuckled as he passed out glasses of the reddish cocktail while Mr. Pennyfather, still gagged, glared daggers at us all. We ignored him. After a thoroughly fruitless round of questioning the man, Aunt Butty had insisted on it, saying it would "soften him up." I was starting to think Chaz was right about the detective films.

The Bishop was an interesting cocktail. The rum was... strong, with just a hint of the fruit coming through from the wine and lime juice, and a bit of sweetness from the simple syrup. I wasn't sure I'd give up my Aviations for it, but it was certainly something different. I could get used to it.

"What the devil is going on here?" Hale walked into the room in his robe and slippers, looking delightfully disheveled, half asleep, and very confused.

"Chaz is making cocktails, darling. Want one?" I leaned over to give him a kiss and let him try a sip of my cocktail.

"Thank you, no. Could do with some coffee, though. Also... why have you got a man tied to a chair?" He didn't seem terribly surprised that there was a man tied up in my sitting room, but he shot me a look as he reached for the bell to summon Maddie.

Before he could ring it, Maddie barged in, half-shouting, "Gentleman to see you, my lady." Her eyes rounded and she stumbled to a halt. "What the—?"

James nearly plowed into the back of her. So much for keeping him out of this. "What the devil?!"

"Yes, yes. We've already been through this. Maddie, please bring coffee for Hale. Hale, James, you'd both better sit down. Chaz, I think James needs a drink."

"James needs several drinks," James muttered, sinking onto the sofa.

"I thought we were keeping him out of it." Louise nodded at James, clutching her drink in one hand and trying to grab Peaches with the other. Peaches was having none of it and hopped up on the window seat, burrowing under the cushions.

Mr. Pennyfather shouted from behind his gag, but it came out a garbled mess. Aunt Butty whacked him on the back of the head with her palm and told him to hush and let the grownups talk.

I just hoped we didn't all end up locked in the Tower after this. Not that they used the Tower for prisoners very often these days, but with our luck, they'd decide that's where we belonged.

"I'm in a mad house," James mumbled. "We're all going to prison."

"You've got that right." Maddie sailed in behind him, her face creased with disapproval as she dropped a tea tray unceremoniously on the table. The coffeepot gave a rattling protest and she glared at it. "Kidnapping. Murder. Shenanigans of all sorts. What will you think of next?" This time I got the glare.

"Thank you, Maddie. Now why don't you head back to the kitchen. You know, plausible deniability and all that," I suggested.

She let out a snort and stomped out. I should probably give her a hefty bonus this Christmas.

"Perhaps we've given Mr. Pennyfather enough softening time," I said to my aunt. "We should try questioning him again."

"Let me." Louise thrust her empty cocktail glass at me and strode toward her husband, ripping his gag out. "Enough of this nonsense, Mortimer. It's time to face facts. Why are you involved in all of these criminal activities?"

Mr. Pennyfather sighed heavily. "Louise, darling, I suggest you release me straightaway, lest I be forced to arrest you along with everyone else."

"Really, Mortimer. Threats? I am your wife. Explain yourself!" Her tone turned imperious.

Alas, Mr. Pennyfather remained unswayed. He refused to answer a single question.

"Are you involved in the theft of the goddess statue from the Museum of Britain?" I demanded.

Nothing.

"Did you have anything to do with Mabel's murder?"

Still nothing.

"Why did you and your men search Mabel's flat?"

Again, nothing.

Even when I asked about getting kidnapped, he had no reaction and made no comment. It was most annoying.

"Nothing for it," Aunt Butty said. "He'll have to stew a bit longer. Put the gag back, Louise."

"Wait a min—"

But poor Mr. Pennyfather didn't have time to finish whatever he was about to say. Louise stuffed the gag back in with far more enthusiasm than was probably warranted.

"He's right, you know," James said. "We could all wind up in prison for this."

"Pish posh." Aunt Butty waved a hand airily. "If he does arrest us, he'll have to admit he was kidnapped by two ladies of a certain age. He'll never do that."

"Chaz and I were there too," I reminded her.

"Louise and I could have handled it on our own," Aunt Butty said airily, adjusting her mauve turban which matched the overly floral kimono. She looked like she should be reading palms, not kidnapping MI5 agents.

"Doubtful," Chaz muttered.

"I heard that." She gave him a sour look.

"It's getting late," I interrupted before they could start another argument. "I, for one, would like to get to bed."

"We should leave a guard on him," Louise suggested. "Just in case. I've been married to him for over four decades, you know. He may not look like much, but he's wily."

Hale's lips twitched, and I nearly burst out laughing.

"I'm probably going to regret this, but I'll take first watch," James offered. "That way I can go home after and hopefully get some sleep."

"Don't be daft," I told him. "You don't need to get involved in this. Plausible deniability, remember? You and Maddie can deny everything."

"That bird has flown the coop," Hale muttered.

"He's right," James said. "I might as well help out."

"Believe me. We have plenty of people to watch over him. In fact, we can lock him in one of the guest rooms. That way everyone can get some sleep."

"You should still tie him down," Louise said. "Wily, remember?"

I remembered. Although I doubted the veracity of her claims.

James insisted on helping Hale and Chaz get Mr. Pennyfather up the stairs and into the guest room where Louise and Aunt Butty immediately pounced. I have no idea where they got the strips of cloth to tie him with, and I was afraid to ask, but they had him tied to the bed posts in a shockingly short amount of time.

"If you're sure you can handle things, I'll be off." James still looked reluctant.

"Go." I shooed him down the hall. "Aunt Butty and Louise have him well and truly in hand. It promises to be a quiet night."

After all, with a house full of guards, what could possibly go wrong?

Shéa MacLeod

Chapter 15

I woke with a start and sat bolt upright in bed. Beside me, Hale muttered something sleepily, so I patted his arm and said, "It's fine. Go back to sleep."

The snoring recommenced immediately.

It was dark out, the sky only just hinting at turning gray at the edges. Far too early for me to be awake. Still, something had woken me. What was it?

Someone tapped softly on my door. I guess that was the "what" in question, but who would be knocking at this time of night?

I slid out of bed, stuffed my feet into slippers, and donned my striped, green silk dressing gown before answering the door. Maddie stood there, hair sticking out like a wild woman and eyes as wide as saucers. "Sorry to disturb, m'lady, but there's been An Incident."

She pronounced the last two words with all the gravity due a murder trial. Unfortunately, my mind was too fuzzy to make any sense of it. "What sort of incident?"

"It's that aunt of yours. And her friend. They—"

I held up my hand. "Say no more. Guest room?"

She nodded. "They said to come straightaway."

"Oh, I plan to." Tightening my robe, I marched down the hall and rapped on the guest room door which cracked open to reveal a single eyeball. "What the deuce is going on in there, Aunt Butty?"

The door opened the rest of the way and my aunt stood there in her nightgown and dark velvet dressing gown, her hair covered by a nightcap that had gone out of fashion thirty years ago. "There you are. We have a... small problem."

"What sort of a small problem?" I asked suspiciously.

She backed up, allowing me to step inside the dim room. At first everything seemed perfectly ordinary. Well, as ordinary as can be when one has a person tied to one's guest bed. The four-poster bed was as old as Methuselah, but I'd replaced the faded bed curtains with a swath of sheer pink organza to match the bed linens and the milk glass lamps on either side.

Louise, also in nightclothes—When had the two of them had time to pack their bags?—stood next to the bed, an antique bedpan clutched in one hand. The window behind her was wide open. At her feet was slumped a man in dark clothing. Since Mr. Pennyfather was still tied up and glaring at me, it certainly wasn't him.

"What happened?" I demanded, nudging the inert form with my toe, then bent down to get a look at his face. I didn't recognize him. He was certainly not one of the men at the museum.

"That man," Aunt Butty pointed dramatically to the still figure on the floor, "broke in here through that window." Another dramatic point at the open window. "He had a knife! I'm certain he was here to murder us all in our beds!"

I found that doubtful, although the fact he was armed was of some consternation. I eyed Louise. "Let me guess. You bashed him over the head with the bed pan."

She shrugged, setting the bedpan down next to Mr. Pennyfather, who was very much awake and very much irritated—if the redness of his face was anything to go by. "It was the only thing to hand. Do calm down, Mortimer. You'll give yourself a fit."

I was fairly certain he was already having a fit of epic proportions, but I focused on the matter at hand which was an unconscious man sprawled on my carpet. Granted, he'd broken in and was thus there illegally, but it wasn't like we could call the police what with the whole kidnapping angle. I could clearly picture North's cheerful expression as he slapped handcuffs on the lot of us.

The man on the floor groaned, and Mr. Pennyfather's gaze went straight to him. I was starting to have a bad feeling about this.

"Louise, I think your husband knows this man," I said.

She glanced from me to the man to her husband, and back again. "Surely not! Mortimer, you cannot possibly know this person!"

Mr. Pennyfather mumbled something from behind his gag. This was getting us nowhere. I strode to his side and undid the knot securing the gag. I was not stupid enough to untie him, though. He might wring my neck. Not that I could blame him. I'd do the same in his position.

"The lot of you have some explaining to do," he snapped, although his words came out a little sticky. Probably from dry mouth.

"Louise, could you give him some water, please? I think he needs some."

"Very well. Although he hardly deserves it. Heavens knows what he's been up to. Sending ruffians after me."

So Louise believed, as I did, that the man on the floor was somehow involved with Mr. Pennyfather. No doubt one of his minions from MI5. Which didn't bode well for us, since we'd koshed him over the head and kidnapped his boss. Well, Louise had done the koshing, but we'd all been in on the kidnapping.

Once Louise had helped her husband take a sip of water, and Aunt Butty had tucked the bed pan back under the bed where it belonged, I decided I'd better get what I could out of Mr. Pennyfather before we were all thrown in prison.

"I take it he's one of yours," I said with a nod to the prone figure who was now starting to stir.

"Yes," Mr. Pennyfather gritted out. "He's one of my men. He came here to free me, no doubt thinking I'd been captured by enemy operatives instead of..." He glanced at us all gathered in our nightclothes and sighed. "Well, whatever *this* is. Louise, have you lost your mind?"

"She hasn't," I assured him, although, honestly, it was debatable. If he thought this was outrageous, he didn't know his wife well. The things she and my aunt got up to... Well, let's just say kidnapping and assault by bed pan were fairly minor. "They were trying to help me."

"Help you?"

"I've been hired by the museum to find a missing artifact," I told him, not bothering to mention James. Probably best to keep at least one of us out of prison.

"You really do honestly think you're a detective, don't you?" He sounded horrified.

I thought about informing him of my great successes so far, but I figured it'd be a waste of my breath. Louise probably already told him anyway. "My investigation led me to Mabel Pierce, one of the museum employees, which led me to her flat and you. I'm sure you recall meeting me there the day you and your troops stormed the place."

His gaze narrowed. "I remember. You were being nosy as usual."

"I'm being paid to be nosy." Well, I wasn't exactly getting paid as far as I knew, but he didn't need to know that.

"Whatever you think you know about me, you're wrong. My investigation has nothing to do with your missing artifact."

"How can you be certain?"

He gave me a look.

"Fine," I huffed. "But if that's so, why are you mucking about in Mabel's murder?"

"Because the murder has nothing to do with your little mystery," he all but shouted.

"Calm down, dear," Louise ordered. "Remember, your heart."

"There is nothing bloody wrong with my heart, woman!" he bellowed. "What is wrong is you bunch of interfering busybodies mucking up my investigation."

Aunt Butty tutted. "That's no way to talk to ladies, Mortimer."

Mr. Pennyfather looked like his head might explode. I felt some sympathy for the man. After all, Aunt Butty could drive a person to drink sometimes. Although he was married to Louise, so he should be used to it.

"Then what's it to do with?" I asked. "If Mabel Pierce wasn't killed because of the stolen goddess statue, why did she die?"

"That, my dear, is a matter of national security." His tone was smug and condescending.

I stopped feeling sorry for him immediately. "Do you honestly expect me to believe that Mabel's murder had nothing to do with the theft?" I didn't buy it. Not for a minute.

Mr. Pennyfather shrugged. Or at least tried to. Aunt Butty and Louise had tied him up very well indeed. "Believe what you will, but my investigation into Miss Pierce has nothing to do with the theft."

I sighed. Wonderful. We were back at square one.

After a great deal of discussion—and more than a few threats from Mr. Pennyfather in regard to the release of both him and his man and what would happen should we not do so immediately—it was left to Louise to deal with her spouse. I have no idea what she said, but the two men left my home under their own power and with their proverbial tails between their legs.

"He'll have us all arrested, mark my words," Maddie muttered darkly as she handed Louise's driver an ancient carpet bag which Louise had stuffed to the brim.

"Not to worry." Louise gave me a knowing look as she exited behind her husband. "I've got things well in hand."

"What's she mean by that?" Maddie asked with a frown.

"It means that as scary as Mr. Pennyfather and his MI5 connections may be, Louise Pennyfather is a great deal scarier," I said.

"Never forget it, young woman." Aunt Butty gave Maddie a pat on the back so hardy it nearly toppled her into the ficus. "A woman of a certain age is not to be trifled with." She righted her sleeping cap which had gone a little limp and off center during all the hubbub. "And the best part is, no one suspects us of anything nefarious. More pity them." She winked. "Now, I'm to bed. Need my beauty sleep, you know."

Maddie shook her head and headed back up to her room, muttering all the way about madhouses and lunatics. I could hardly blame her. She'd led a rather ordinary and respectable life until she came to me. She'd no idea that being my maid would involve murder, mayhem, and general shenanigans. And she certainly didn't approve.

I caught myself on a yawn. It was almost five in the morning and, while I'd a habit of staying up late and sleeping in, events were catching up to me.

As I slowly climbed the stairs, my conversation with Mr. Pennyfather replayed in my mind. I laughed softly with amusement, remembering his outrage at Louise cold cocking the MI5 agent with a bed pan. Honestly, Aunt Butty should forget trying to write fiction—her latest obsession—and stick with her autobiography. It was far stranger than anything anyone could make up.

Then it hit me. I paused mid-step. Something Mr. Pennyfather had said. He hadn't said he wasn't investigating Mabel, though he'd allowed me to think so, but he'd been very clear that her *death* wasn't related to my investigation. In other words, the thefts. Only I didn't buy it.

Mabel may have been involved in whatever it was Mr. Pennyfather was investigating, but I was absolutely convinced her death was related to the theft of the artifact. Or even multiple artifacts, if Mabel's claims were correct.

I dashed upstairs and dug out Mabel's notebook and journal from where I'd hidden them at the bottom of my wardrobe. Returning to the sitting room, I plopped down on the sofa and flipped through first the diary, and then the notebook, matching up dates and notations and trying to make sense of things. At last, I found something.

Overheard Mr. X. Next exchange on full moon.

That was it. There was nothing else, but I knew in my bones the exchange referred to was of a stolen artifact. What Mabel had planned to do about it, I'd no idea, but I knew I needed a plan. Because the next full moon she referred to was tomorrow night!

And *that* meant we weren't back to square one at all.

In fact, this just sent the case on a whole new trajectory!

Chapter 16

"You want to do what?" James looked at me like I'd gone batty.

I'd told them what I'd found in Mabel's writings. They'd both agreed it wasn't enough to take to the police, but it was enough for a stakeout.

"Oh, trust me, this is nothing," Chaz drawled. "She once tried to break into a jewelry store in Paris."

"She once actually *did* break into a jewelry store in Paris," I said tartly.

He winked at me then turned back to James. "Ophelia has more lives than a cat. She'll be fine."

"And if she isn't?" James fumed.

"Then we'll be there as backup, dear boy." Chaz flung his arm around James' neck which turned as red as his face. Chaz's grin widened. They were too adorable.

"Fine," James muttered. "We'll be there as backup. But I don't like it."

"Because I'm female?" I gave him a warning look.

"Because you're a civilian. You haven't been trained to protect yourself."

"Yes, I have. I went to Louise Pennyfather's Art of the Bedpan. I'm fairly certain Aunt Butty taught her that move, by the by."

Chaz laughed, and James rolled his eyes. They really were too cute.

"In all seriousness, I have learned several tricks over the years, so don't fret about me. The issue at hand is, how do I get into the museum without anyone finding out?"

"We can have Mr. Evans get you a position on staff," James suggested.

I shook my head. "That'll take time. Besides, I don't want anyone knowing I'm there. Not even Mr. Evans. I'm not entirely sure I trust the man. After all, the artifacts have all gone missing on his watch." I tapped my chin in thought. "I've got it. I'll go in undercover as a cleaning woman."

Chaz snorted with laughter. "You will never pass as a cleaning woman, old thing."

"Ah, that's where you're wrong." I whipped one of Maddie's voluminous dusting aprons and an old bit of cloth off the sofa and wrapped myself in them. The cloth covered my hair, and the apron hid practically everything else. I even hunched over and squinted just a touch as if I were nearsighted.

"Well, I'll be," James murmured. "That'll do it."

"You'll have to wear different shoes," Chaz said, staring pointedly at my strappy sandals which were more appropriate to a Sunday picnic in the park than to scrubbing floors.

"Of course. Don't be daft. I've got an old pair of brogues that'll work perfectly."

"And how do you plan to get in?" James crossed his arms over his chest.

"We already know from our investigation that the bulk of the cleaning women arrive just as the museum is closing. They spend a few hours cleaning, then vacate the premises. I'll slip in with them."

He mulled it over. "The women will obviously notice that you're not one of the usual cleaners."

"Sure, but I can say I'm new. They must get new people now and then."

He grimaced. "I don't like it."

"Don't worry. I'll try and avoid being noticed by them as much as possible. Head down, polish the floor, whatever."

Chaz grinned. "And then what?"

"Soon as I can, I'll slip off and hide somewhere. A cupboard or office. Maybe even Mabel's office, since no one is using it. Once the cleaners leave, I'll poke around and see what I can find. If I read Mabel's diary correctly, tonight is a pickup night for the thieves. We can finally discover who they are. Depending on how things go, we follow them and find out where they're holed up. Then we make an anonymous call to the police, and Bob's your uncle."

"Too many American films, just like Aunt Butty," Chaz chortled.

I ignored him. Although he may be onto something. Although in my case it was more Agatha Christie novels than gangster films.

"And if something goes wrong?" James demanded, ignoring Chaz's glee.

"Then I'll scream my head off, and the two of you come running."

The plan worked like a breeze. At least to start.

It was easy enough to slip in behind the line of cleaning women, shoulders bent, head ducked, completely covered in the voluminous apron. I looked just like one of them, and no one paid me any mind, least of all the guards. Even the other cleaners didn't pay me any mind. Someone asked about Ethel and was informed she was out sick. I suppose they assumed I was her replacement for the night.

Once we hit the lobby, everyone spread out, each woman seeming to know exactly where to go. I had no idea where I would be expected to clean, so I set out with purpose just like the others, heading toward the storage area and the offices. I figured that was the best bet for a meetup of criminals, since that's where the bulk of the artifacts were stored and it was away from the main areas of the museum where the guards no doubt spent the bulk of their patrols.

In fact, the previous thefts had all come from the storage area, only coming to light after several days, weeks, or even months when they were supposed to be brought out for cleaning and study. The goddess statue was oddly the only item to deviate from that pattern.

Which begged the question, were the thieves the same? I was betting so. After all, it would be quite the coincidence to have two sets of thieves running around one museum. Not out of the question, but unlikely. No, I was betting something had gone wrong and forced them to improvise.

Before I could reach my intended target, I heard male voices. The guards! I ducked into the nearest unlocked door which happened to be a broom cupboard, although apparently not one in frequent use as it was crammed with dusty boxes and old empty cleaning fluid bottles.

I waited until the voices passed before poking my head out to see if the coast was clear. It was not. More voices. I must be close to the guards' room, and no doubt it was time for their rounds. I ducked back in, pulling the door shut behind me.

Once the next set of guards passed by, I glanced at the watch pinned to Maddie's apron and noted the time, knowing the amount of time between rounds would be invaluable information to avoid being caught. I then went about making myself somewhere to sit. I was able to quietly move some boxes to create a makeshift chair, then settled down to wait.

About a half hour later, the guards trickled back, their voices and footsteps once more echoing in the hall as they headed toward their room. Right, a half hour for rounds, but how much time between? And when would the cleaning crew leave? I'd no doubt that any pickup would take place after the cleaning women left and between the guards' rounds when they were all back in their room doing... whatever it was they did. That would be the safest time for nefarious goings-on.

Approximately an hour and a half went by before the guards exited their room again, peeling off into various parts of the museum. I counted six. Which didn't seem many for such a large place. Then again, this was the night shift, and they didn't have to worry about patrons and sticky fingers—only to ensure there were no break-ins. Although clearly break-ins weren't the biggest problem around here.

About the same time the guards finished their rounds, the chatter of women's voices echoed from out in the rotunda, then down the hall, past my hiding place. The cleaners were done for the night. They bid goodbye to the guards—no one had marked my absence among them—then all was quiet.

I glanced at my watch again. An hour and a half until the next round. Plenty of time to move into the storage area.

Leaving my mop and bucket behind, I slipped out of the closet, carefully shutting it behind me. It was dark in the museum; all the lights were out. The only illumination came from pale moonlight spilling through high windows, and golden lamplight pouring into the hall from the open guards' room door. I needed to pass that room to get to my destination.

There was no way I'd be able to move silently in the leather-soled brogues that were part of my disguise, so I slid them off and clutched them in one hand. In stockinged feet, I edged toward the spill of light and the chatter of male voices. Curls of cigar smoke edged the open doorway. Why couldn't they have shut it? It would have made my life so much easier.

I peered cautiously around the door frame. Five of the guards were huddled around a table, smoking and playing cards. The sixth was sprawled on a ratty old sofa, his uniform jacket open and his hat over his face as he napped. I didn't need to worry about him.

Since everyone else's attention was focused on the card game, I moved to the far side of the hall, took a deep breath, and slipped across. I half expected someone to shout after me, but no one did. I let out a soft sigh of relief and picked up the pace.

Once I reached the storage room, I slipped my shoes back on. I'd no idea what obstacles lay in my path, and I didn't want to break a toe or sprain an ankle. I'd just have to tiptoe and hope no one heard me.

The storage room was dark as a tomb, just like before. Awkward shapes huddled an even darker shade against the black. The tiny windows high up barely illuminated anything as I picked my way cautiously through the maze toward where I knew the employee offices and labs lay.

I finally reached the hall which held Mabel's office and let out a sigh of relief. At least there was nothing here to run into. I was about to enter Mabel's office when I noticed a faint line of light streaming under the door of an office further down. Someone was here! It could be a coincidence, someone working late, or it could be the criminals!

I hurried down the hall to the door which was, unfortunately, closed. Pressing my ear to it, I could hear the faint murmur of voices, but I couldn't make out what they were saying. Then footsteps headed toward the door.

Whirling, I ran back down the hall and darted into Mabel's office just as the door opened and a man exited. He was a large man in a tan overcoat and fedora, clutching a wrapped object.

Behind him was a second man, this one with a manilla envelope in his hand. "You're sure it's all here?"

"Every last dime. Nice doing business with you." The large man lifted his hat mockingly, I thought. I recognized him immediately as one of the men who'd been speaking with Mr. Pennyfather. The same man who'd held a gun to me. The man with the pockmarked face.

The second man stepped fully into the doorway. My jaw dropped and I clapped my hand over my mouth to avoid them hearing my gasp. I recognized him, too. It was Dr. Foster.

Chapter 17

The two men shook hands, and I swear I wanted to wipe the gloating expressions from their smug faces. How dare they use their positions to steal from the museum!

It was clear to me now that Dr. Foster was the Mr. X in Mabel's diary. He was the one helping the thief steal artifacts. No doubt if I searched Foster's office, I'd find Mabel's missing files.

They walked to the end of the hall where Dr. Foster opened the employee entrance so the crooked MI5 agent could exit. He then turned and walked slowly back to his office, counting the money in the envelope. I could confront him, or I could follow the agent. Well, I knew who Dr. Foster was and where he'd be, so I figured I should follow the agent and find out where he went.

I tried not to tap my foot impatiently as I waited for Foster to get out of the way. Finally, he reentered his office and shut the door.

I let out a sigh of relief and hurried down the hall to the exit and cautiously opened the door a crack to peer outside. I couldn't see anybody, so I dashed out the door, closing it softly behind me, and then hurried to the pavement. A glance left and right, and I spotted the MI5 agent climbing into an old beat-up vehicle. Now what? I could hardly follow him on foot.

"Where the devil is James?" I muttered to myself as the engine on the car revved.

"Right here," said a low voice, and James stepped out from the shadows, nearly giving me apoplexy. "Chaz has the car running. Come on." He grabbed my hand, and we ran for Chaz's car which idled at the curb, clambering into the backseat.

"Follow that car!" I all but shouted. I'd always wanted to say that.

Chaz chuckled and pulled out into the street, his headlamps off. "I know it's a risk, but this way he won't see us. Hopefully."

I nodded. "Good thinking."

Chaz careened through the streets, hot on the tail of our quarry. Fortunately, it was late and there wasn't much traffic, otherwise we might have been in a bit of a pickle what with having no head lamps. As it was, we managed to follow the agent to a small house on the outskirts of London.

Chaz pulled to the curb as the agent parked in the drive next to the ordinary, but fairly new, semi-detached house. Lights were on, so someone was home. He climbed out of the car, the bundle he'd taken from the museum tucked in one arm, whistling casually like he'd all the time in the world and nothing to worry about. He strolled right up to the front door and let himself in, closing the door behind him.

"That must be where he lives," I said.

"Seems dangerous to keep stolen goods in the family home," Chaz mused.

"Good cover," James said. "Who'd think a family man living on the outskirts of London would be dealing in stolen artifacts?"

I opened the door and stuck one leg out of the car.

James grabbed my arm. "What do you think you're doing?"

"Getting a closer look." I shrugged him off and slid out, closing the door before he could argue further. Really, you'd think I'd never done this before.

"I'm coming with you." Chaz jumped out, too. "A good detective always takes backup."

I leaned in the open window and spoke to James. "Keep the car running. Just in case."

"If anyone's going, it should be me," James argued. "I am, after all, the one trained in such things."

Chaz snorted. "Please, I've been on enough stakeouts with Ophelia, I'm more qualified than anyone."

Without waiting for James to argue further, we grabbed each other's hands and dashed for the house. Behind us, James grumbled under his breath as he climbed into the driver's seat. Something about "lunatics" and "Bedlam." While more than one person would agree with his assessment of lunacy, I hardly thought we were deserving of Bedlam.

Curtains had been pulled tight across the front of the house, so we slunk around the side, looking for somewhere to peer in. We were rewarded with a narrow window covered only by a roller shade which hadn't been pulled down properly. There was a three- or four-inch gap at the bottom, giving us a good view into what appeared to be a kitchen.

A woman of about thirty or so stood at the range, stirring something in a pot. I couldn't tell what it was, but the aroma of sautéing onions permeated the neighborhood. Apparently, it was supper time all around.

The pockmarked agent entered the kitchen, dropped a kiss on the woman's head, and then disappeared through a door. It seemed strange that a man who'd held me at gunpoint would be so tender with his wife. But I supposed even criminals loved their families.

"Where do you suppose that door goes?" Chaz whispered. "Cellar perhaps?"

I shook my head. "These newer semi-detached houses don't have cellars. Too expensive to dig." Unlike my townhouse which had a ground level that was half underground, very common in my older neighborhood. "I'm guessing it's a pantry or some other type of storage closet."

"Or perhaps an office," Chaz suggested.

"Could be." Although the house was a bit small for that. Still, they could have turned some other room into an office, I supposed.

Pockmark wasn't gone long and, when he returned, he no longer held the package. He sat at the kitchen table and picked up a newspaper, while the woman paused in her stirring to pour him a glass of beer.

I yanked on Chaz's coat sleeve, urging him to follow me. We stayed low as we edged around the house, across the back garden and toward the part of the house where the agent had disappeared to. Hopefully there would be a window into whatever room or closet he'd stored the package.

As we approached the part of the house closest to the neighboring fence, a dog barked next door. Loud, obnoxious, and clearly out for our blood. Before we could reach our destination, the back porch light next door snapped on. If we were caught—

Without saying a word, we bolted back across the garden and down the side of the house toward the street. Voices echoed from behind us as we dashed across the pavement and dove into the car's backseat, shouting, "Go! Go! Go!"

James went, revving the engine and tearing down the street like the proverbial bat out of Hell.

I squeezed my eyes shut and prayed Pockmark hadn't seen us.

Although James demanded several times to know what had happened, we waited until we were safely back at my place to tell him everything. It helped that we were fortified with stiff drinks.

"Hopefully our quarry didn't realize that the interlopers in his back garden were related to his own theft," Chaz moaned.

"Doubtful," James assured him. "They didn't see you after all."

"How do you know?" I asked.

He shrugged. "No one appeared in sight while I was waiting for you. If they'd have been in a position to spot you racing back to the car, I'd have seen them."

"Fair enough," I said, leaning back with a sigh. "Now what? We've got no proof Pockmark stole anything, and Mr. Pennyfather is never going to believe one of his men is involved in this. Especially not after he was our—ah—guest."

"You mean kidnap victim," Hale said dryly as he entered the sitting room. "Hello, love." He leaned down to kiss me.

I kissed him back with some enthusiasm. "You're home early."

"No, you're up late," he teased, then glanced at the drink in my hand. "Don't suppose I could wrangle one of those."

"I'll fix you one, old chap," Chaz said, jumping from his chair and draining his own drink. "I could use a refill. Anyone else?"

While he fixed fresh drinks, James and I caught Hale up on the evening's shenanigans. Up to and including our nearly getting caught by the dirty MI5 agent who I was calling Pockmark, for obvious reasons.

"I can't believe it was Foster all along," I said, taking a long swallow of my cocktail. "I was sure it was Evans."

"Don't forget that Dr. Prentiss, the dinosaur man, told us that Mabel and Foster didn't get along," James pointed out. "That Foster was constantly undermining her. Sounds like he was telling the truth."

"You're right. And it was Foster who told us about Mabel's anger over not getting funding for her research. Question at hand is, what do we do now?" I asked. "How can we prove that both Pockmark and Dr. Foster are in this up to their eyeballs?"

"The agent is easy," Hale said, taking the cocktail Chaz offered. "The stolen property is right there in his house, correct?"

The three of us nodded in unison.

"Well, then, a simple anonymous call to the police as you originally planned. Stolen artifacts found—or one anyway—the agent and Dr. Foster arrested. There you have it. Happens all the time back home."

I nodded in approval. "That's a good plan. But how do we prove to the police Dr. Foster is involved? He may have unaccounted cash on him, but no doubt he can just claim it's a donation or something. There's no way to prove he was paid for the artifacts or involved in their theft."

"Pockmark might put the finger on him," Chaz said with a chuckle. "I have always wanted to say that!"

"Now who's been watching too many American films?" I said dryly.

"There's no way a hardened agent like Pockmark will flip." James snapped his fingers. "We'll have to get Foster to confess."

"I'm not sure it will be that easy. He's not the sort of person to blab, either. And I'm still not convinced Evans isn't involved." Perhaps I was being stubborn on that point, but I felt it in my bones.

"So we question Evans," James said. "He should be easy enough to break. He seemed a bit high strung."

I certainly agreed with that assessment.

"And once we get him to confess, Evans and Foster will turn on each other." Chaz grinned. "Followed by our crooked agent, Pockmark. Down like a row of dominoes. Delightful! And once again, Lady Rample and Company save the day! Cheers!" He raised his glass.

"So much for Woodward and Company," James muttered low enough only I could hear him.

I held back a snicker. He'd get used to it if he was going to hang around Chaz and me for any length of time.

"North will never listen to me," I pointed out. Our history was fraught, to say the least.

"That's why it should be an anonymous phone call," James said.

"Forget that," Chaz said. "You should have Louise do it. He'll have to listen to someone like Louise. She's *connected*."

I didn't point out that I was also connected. Truth was, Louise's connections far outstripped mine. "She's also on the board. She could tell North she uncovered the theft in her capacity as a board member. Based on the information in Mabel's diary, previous thefts weren't reported until days or even weeks after the artifacts went missing."

"To make it easier for the thieves to cover their tracks," James mused.

"Exactly. If Louise reports the theft to North before Mr. Evans does, it'll be difficult for him to get around that." I grinned. "How could he explain not reporting a theft? And easier for us to get an admission of guilt. Especially when North raids Pockmark's house and finds the exact item Louise reported stolen."

"Perfect," Hale said, standing. "Wish I could be a fly on the wall for that conversation, but I need to get to bed."

"As do the rest of us," James agreed. "It's been a long night, and it'll be hours yet before we can put our plan into action."

I wanted to get going right that minute, but he was right. Louise would still be abed and not appreciate my calling in the middle of the night. Not to mention, the museum didn't open until late morning, so it would no doubt be some time before Mr. Evans or Dr. Foster put in an appearance.

James and Chaz bid us goodnight and left, and I followed Hale up to bed. The morning would come early enough, I supposed. Still, my mind was awhirl even as my head hit the pillow. I doubted I would sleep a wink.

Chapter 18

Maddie all but shook me awake the next morning. Hale was still sound asleep, and the draperies drawn so the room was dark and cool, her face but a pale oval hanging above me like a bad omen.

I glared up at her, bleary eyed and with a caustic comment on my tongue. She hadn't even brought coffee! Or tea! But she pressed a finger to her lips and held out my silk dressing gown.

With a sigh, I heaved myself out of bed and allowed her to wrap me in the gown while I shoved bare feet into felt loafer slippers with pompoms in the same green color as the gown. I yawned as I followed Maddie out into the hall, carefully closing the door behind me.

Once we were some distance down the hall, I said, "What's going on?"

"Mr. Woodward and Mr. Chaz are here, m'lady. They said I ought to get you up straight away so as you could put the plan into action." She made a face. She clearly did not approve.

"Ah, yes, the plan." I yawned again. "Please tell me you've got coffee ready."

"Of course." She huffed an annoyed sigh. "It's in the sitting room. I didn't want to wake up Mr. Hale."

Right. Of course not. Maddie thought the sun shone out of Hale's backside. Not so much mine.

"Thank you, Maddie."

"If that's all, I'll be in the kitchen."

"Not baking, I hope," I said with some horror.

"Don't be daft. I'm doing dishes."

As promised, Chaz and James awaited me in the sitting room, already drinking their coffee. I walked straight to the pot and fixed myself a cup, waiting to speak until I took that first, blissful sip.

Once so fortified, I turned to face my guests. "Good morning, gentlemen. Are we ready to put our plan into action?"

"Ready when you are, old thing," Chaz said far too cheerfully for this hour of the morning.

"You think Mrs. Pennyfather will be out of bed?" James asked.

"Louise? She's an early riser." At least compared to yours truly. "She's probably been up for hours. I'll make the call."

Coffee in hand, I strode to the telephone and rang Louise Pennyfather. Once I told her what we needed her to do, she was over the moon to be involved.

"Happy to help, my darling," she boomed. "Shall I ring this North person straight away?"

"If you would, Louise. Thanks. And let me know what he says?"

"Of course. I'll ring you straight back."

I hung up the phone and turned to face the boys. "She's on it."

It was, perhaps, a good twenty minutes and much pacing later before Louise called. It had taken her some time to get put through to North, but she'd played her part to the hilt, and he had promised to meet her at the museum in two hours. *After* a visit to Pockmark's house.

"I had to do some heavy lifting there, my girl. Had to come up with some explanation as to how I knew this Pockmark person had the stolen artifact."

Oh, dear. "What did you tell him?"

"That I'd seen him, of course, and gotten his address from my husband. Easy-peasy. I'll meet you at the museum, shall I?"

Which meant I'd need to hustle to get ready in time to meet her there. My presence would no doubt be an unpleasant surprise for Detective Inspector North. I couldn't wait to see the expression on his face!

After downing a quick breakfast of bacon sandwiches—one of the few things Maddie could make with any competency—I left Chaz and James to their own devices while I dashed upstairs to get dressed. I chose a red Chanel suit that fit me like a glove and made me feel... powerful. It was the sort of suit which, when worn with the proper attitude, caused people to take one seriously. In this case, hopefully North would do so.

Once properly attired, I joined Chaz and James on the drive to the museum. Chaz had insisted on driving, as he claimed I drove like a drunk llama. It was a ridiculous claim as I am certain llamas can't drive even when sober.

Louise met us on the front steps of the museum. Like me, she wore a Chanel suit. Unlike mine which was a solid color that went well with my skin tone, hers was a garishly loud tartan plaid print in green, yellow, orange, and brown that made her skin look sallow. Peaches was on a lead clipped to a collar of the same print. I was certain dogs weren't allowed inside. I was equally certain no one would dare stop Louise bringing along her precious pet. No one in their right mind would ever say no to Louise Pennyfather.

We found Mr. Evans in his office, finishing a cup of tea. He looked somewhat non-plussed to see the four of us. He patted his lips tidily with a cloth napkin. "Did we have an appointment?"

Louise pushed her way to the front. "I need a word with you, Harry."

"Ah, Mrs. Pennyfather. Lovely to have a board member here at any time," he said, rising, brushing at his gray suit as if to remove wrinkles or crumbs. He did that a lot. "How may I help?"

"You can tell me why several artifacts from this museum have gone missing," Louise said, looming over poor Harry who turned a little pale.

"Well, as you know, Mrs. Pennyfather, I have reported those thefts to the police—"

"Not those thefts. The others." She glared at him, and Peaches let out a little accusatorial bark for good measure.

"I assure you, Mrs. Pennyfather, only a couple of items have been taken and those have been duly reported to the authorities as per protocol." This time he used the napkin to blot the sweat beading on his forehead.

"You mean, like this?" Detective Inspector North shoved his way through the crowded office. I hadn't even seen him arrive. He gave me a smug look—not sure why—and pulled a wrapped object from his coat pocket which he unrolled. A gold ankh dropped onto the desk with a thud. "I believe this belongs to the museum."

"Wh-where did you find that?" Mr. Evans was shaking so bad he had to sit down.

"In the lair of your accomplice, Mr. Evans." North grew even more smug. "One Agent Darrow."

Ah, so that was Pockmark's name.

"What do you mean my accomplice? I don't know an Agent Darrow. I-I didn't even know the ankh was missing," Mr. Evans insisted.

"Don't lie, Harry," Louise snapped. "We are on to your little game." She'd been watching those gangster films with Aunt Butty.

"Fine! Fine!" He slumped in his chair, a broken man. Look at me being poetic. "But it's not what you think!"

"What is it then?" I demanded.

He mopped his forehead again. "Is it hot in here? I feel overly warm. I don't like the heat." He fanned himself with a file from his desk.

"Evans." Detective Inspector North's voice held a warning note.

"Listen, I wasn't involved in the thefts. Not at all. I had nothing to do with it until after the fact."

"I think you'd better explain, Harry," Louise said.

"What do you want to know?" He twisted the now damp handkerchief.

"Where the rest of the goods are," North said.

"How'd it start?" James said.

"What else have you stolen?" I asked.

The three of us shot each other glares while Chaz and Louise looked bemused. Harry Evans just looked even more broken. He put his head in his hands and moaned.

"None of that, Harry," Louise barked. "You've made your bed and now you must lie upon it."

"She knows that's not how it goes, doesn't she?" Chaz muttered.

I didn't bother to answer. Instead, I focused on Mr. Evans. "How did it start, Harry?"

He swallowed. "Six months ago, I got myself into a bit of bother financially."

"Gambling," James guessed.

Harry nodded miserably. "I didn't have the money and I knew if I didn't pay—" He swallowed even harder. "Well, it wasn't a good idea not to pay if you get my meaning."

I was betting broken limbs would be the least of his worries. Ha. Betting. I amused even myself sometimes.

"Go on," I prodded.

North muttered something about the lunatics running the asylum. We all ignored him. It wasn't the first time we'd heard that in the last twenty-four hours.

"There was no way I could ever come up with the money. I thought of everything... a loan, selling off some of my possessions. And then I lit on an idea." He wrung his hands. "Did you know that only one percent of the museum's artifacts are on display at any given time? One percent! Thousands upon thousands of artifacts just packed away in crates, never to see the light of day. Most of them haven't even been studied."

"So you thought if one or two went missing, no one would be the wiser," I mused. "Particularly if they were from deep within storage, long forgotten."

He nodded. "That was the initial plan, yes. But then I discovered that several pieces were already missing. I was able to contact a dealer I know who told me the items had been sold and by whom." He shifted uneasily.

"Dr. Foster," I said.

He swallowed. "Yes. I needed money desperately, so rather than steal items myself—that just made me far too nervous—I approached Dr. Foster and told him that, for a small fee to cover my debts, I would... turn a blind eye."

"But it became more than that," Chaz guessed.

"It seemed so harmless at first. A little artifact here or there that no one would miss. I would falsify records, move around boxes. Anything to prevent the truth getting out. I got my cut. No one the wiser."

"What went wrong?" North asked, squinted at Harry Evans.

The chair squeaked in protest as Harry leaned back, a look of resignation on his face. "Mr. Pennyfather showed up one day with his agents. Said they were investigating. National security and all that. Wouldn't say what or why, but I was worried that somehow, they'd found out about the thefts and my cover up." He shook his head. "After a while, I realized that they didn't know or care about any missing artifacts—they were focused on something else entirely. I never did figure out what." The what, no doubt, were the secrets being smuggled in and out of the museum. "In any case, things went on as usual. Only someone found out. Dr. Foster was approached by one of the agents, Darrow, who made him, and by extension me, an offer."

"Let me guess," North said. "Deal him in or he'd turn you in."

Harry gripped the edge of the desk, knuckles turning white. "Yes. Only he wanted to take bigger and more expensive things. Foster tried to satisfy him with more of the things in storage, but then Darrow spotted the goddess statue, and he wanted it. I told them they couldn't take it. That it didn't belong to the museum, and it would be noticed."

"But Foster took it anyway," Louise said. "With that ridiculous heist of his."

Harry shrugged. "It worked, but it was obvious that it had been stolen. There was no hiding it. I was forced to bring in outsiders. I had hoped that when they didn't uncover the thief, they would... go away."

"And Mabel?" I asked.

"I don't know how, but she found out about the... deal. She threatened the three of us. Said we needed to return the items, or she'd turn us in."

"She demanded money?" James asked with surprise.

Harry shook his head. "It's not like you think. She didn't care about money. She cared about the artifacts, history. All that. But she had plans, and the museum wouldn't fund her research, so she wanted just enough money for that. She said she'd keep her mouth shut, but only if they stopped stealing and I stopped covering for them."

Interesting. On the one hand she was helping Mr. Pennyfather's investigation and on the other, blackmailing criminals. She clearly was willing to do underhanded things for money, as long as she felt the motive was right and just, but she wasn't willing to allow thefts of artifacts to continue.

"The three of you couldn't stop though," I murmured.

He shook his head. "Foster and Darrow refused. Liked the money too much. Darrow said MI5 didn't pay enough, and he needed it for his retirement. Foster has expensive tastes and a mistress."

"Who killed Mabel Pierce?" Detective Inspector North barked.

"Darrow did," Harry insisted with a shudder. "I could never kill anyone. I didn't even think it was necessary, only he said as long as she knew the truth, we would always be looking over our shoulders."

"Harry Evans, you are under arrest," North said. "And don't worry, Dr. Foster is already in custody, and we'll get your other friend, too."

Harry blanched. "Darrow isn't in custody?"

North grimaced. "He fled when we arrived. Don't worry, though. We'll find him."

"You'd better," Harry said grimly. "Until you do, we're all in danger."

"What do you mean?" James demanded.

Harry gave each of us a long look. "You think he'll go to jail willingly? You better believe Darrow will kill anyone who knows the truth. And that's everyone in this room."

"Oh, dear," said Louise faintly. "*Everyone* in this room?"

"And not only us," I said in horror. "But Aunt Butty, too. And Maddie."

Louise let out a shriek. "And Mortimer!"

Chapter 19

Within minutes we were all piled into our cars—minus Mr. Evans who was taken to the police station by a uniformed officer. Even Detective Inspector North joined us, although I wasn't sure Mr. Pennyfather would appreciate it.

We must have looked an odd caravan as my gorgeous cobalt blue Mercedes Roadster zoomed in and out of traffic, followed closely by North's comparatively staid looking police vehicle, siren blaring, and behind that, Louise's enormous black Bucciali which sailed along like an elegant grand dame. The fact that we nearly plowed over more than one pedestrian meant we'd no doubt appear in tomorrow's paper.

At last, we arrived at the Pennyfather's home. I'd have barged straight in, but North managed to jump in front of us, holding up his hands. "This is police business."

"Poppycock." Louise all but barreled over him, thrusting open the front door, and shouting "Mortimer!" at the top of her lungs.

Before anyone could make a move, Aunt Butty's Bentley pulled to the curb and my aunt climbed out, straightening her puce colored hat which was wildly adorned with mauve and lavender tulle and feathers. It clashed rather badly with her orange and yellow floral dress. Her driver, Simon, was close on her heels, his chauffeur uniform cap set at a jaunty angle.

"We have arrived," Aunt Butty declared dramatically and completely unnecessarily.

"We're in the midst of stopping a tragedy, Aunt Butty, stay here," I ordered.

"That's why we're here. Louise sent over a note this morning, explaining everything. We're here to help. So exciting! Simon, go around back and stop any ruffians from entering."

"Yes, m'lady." He doffed his cap and jogged around the house toward the back garden.

"What the devil is the meaning of this?" North bellowed.

"Best to just go with it," I said, brushing past him. "If you stop for an explanation, poor Mr. Pennyfather will be murdered in his bed before you get through it."

I left him sputtering behind me as I dashed into the house, James and Chaz on my heels. Aunt Butty followed at a more sedate pace. She was not one to throw herself in front of danger if there were younger people available to do so. She would, however, be happy to bask in the glory afterward.

We poked our heads into each doorway, but there was no sign of Louise or Mr. Pennyfather, nor anyone else for that matter. Where could they be?

A shriek echoed through the house. Louise!

"It came from upstairs," Chaz said, taking the steps two at a time.

James and I quickly followed, rushing through the upstairs hall until we came to an open door. It looked to be a study. Inside, Mr. Pennyfather was once again tied to a chair—that was becoming a bad habit of his—Louise was untied but sat in a chair next to him, looking terrified, Peaches cowering next to her, and Chaz stood with his hands up. That's what he got for rushing in.

I grabbed James' sleeve and yanked him to the side before the gunman spotted him. "That's the pockmarked guy we saw talking to Mr. Pennyfather at the museum. The guy who kidnapped me. Agent Darrow."

"Yes, I recognized him, too," he said grimly. "Obviously, Mr. Fosters' accomplice."

I nodded. "Indeed. We need a distraction—"

Before I could finish the thought, something crashed through the study window, shattering the glass. Darrow whirled, his back to us, as a large rock plopped unceremoniously onto the carpet in a shower of window shards.

Without a second thought, I dashed across the room and flung myself upon his back, wrapping my legs about his waist and one arm about his neck. I grabbed his gun arm with my other hand, wrenching it up.

The gun went off with a deafening roar. A chunk of plaster broke loose from the ceiling and dropped straight on Darrow's head, knocking him half senseless. Down we both went, crashing into the floor with me on top. He let out a moan as James ran over and disarmed him.

"That's what you get for terrorizing innocent people," I said, giving the back of his head an extra thump for good measure.

"No need to hit him, Ophelia," James chastised me. "He's pretty well out of it already."

"Oh, there's definitely a need," I assured him, climbing rather inelegantly off the gunman's back. "I find myself highly annoyed at him."

While Chaz freed Mr. Pennyfather and James checked on Louise, North arrived to take custody of

Agent Darrow—aka Pockmark—Aunt Butty hot on his heels. She bustled over to Louise and took charge, cooing and carrying on. No one bothered to check on me. Good thing I was made of sterner stuff.

Curious, I sauntered over to the window and glanced out the gaping hole. Sure enough, Simon grinned up at me. I gave him a wave and he waved back, doffing his cap.

"Alright up there?" he shouted.

"Perfectly splendid," I called back. "Don't you have a date with Maddie today?"

He shrugged. "Your aunt required my assistance."

"And I thank you for it, but don't worry. Go on. I'll get her home."

He waved his thanks and jogged around the corner of the house and out of sight. I turned back to the room and breathed a sigh of relief. Darrow was in custody, no one was injured, and everyone looked to be in remarkably good spirits. All's well that ends well. Or so they say.

Chapter 20

"You won't be able to tell anyone the full truth, of course." Mortimer Pennyfather gave me a long look. He may appear a harmless sort, but I'd no doubt now the man had skills I couldn't even fathom. Getting on his bad side was not on my agenda.

"Of course," I agreed. "Security of the empire and all of that."

"Indeed." He strummed his fingers on the desktop. We were in his office, finally having that meeting we were supposed to have days ago. Only now I knew far more than he ever wanted me to. And he didn't like it. "No one can know the truth behind Mabel Pierce's true involvement in this business."

"Or that of your agent," I said wryly. Not only had the most recent stolen artifact—the ankh—been recovered from Darrow's home, but Detective Inspector North had also found the goddess statue and the address of Fosters' dealer where more artifacts had been retrieved.

"It's for the best," he assured me. "Miss Pierce did a great service for the empire, helping me to uncover a network of spies passing secrets through the museum. Despite her propensity for blackmailing criminals, she did a great deal to protect this country and her own. Unfortunately, if that were made public, the wrong people would find out and we'd lose any advantage we currently have. As far as the public thinks, it is she who was behind the thefts, and she was killed by an unknown partner. With the most valuable of the artifacts returned, including the goddess statue, no one will much care that her so-called partner has disappeared or that a few minor pieces no one has ever seen are missing."

He had a point. "Let me guess, you were at Mabel Pierce's flat that day to recover any evidence she'd gathered on your behalf."

"Indeed. Only someone else got there first." He gave me a knowing look.

"Yes, about that." I pulled both Mabel's diary and what I thought of as her spy notebook from my oversized handbag and slid them across the desk. "Perhaps this will help. Many of her entries are coded, but I made notes about what I've deciphered so far."

"Thank you, my lady. Much appreciated." He tucked both books away. No doubt he'd have experts pouring over them the moment I left.

"And Mr. Evans? What will happen to him? He might not have actively participated in the thefts or the smuggling, but he helped cover it up. Surely, he should be held to account for that."

"If he went to trial, unfortunately everything would come out. And, once again, that would mean revealing certain ongoing operations that might endanger the country."

I sighed. There was nothing so annoying as people getting away with protecting a murderer for the so-called greater good. "He has to pay. He can't just get away with this."

"No, he cannot. Don't worry." A sly smile spread across Mr. Pennyfather's face. "He has been... promoted."

"What?" I all but screeched. "That's hardly right!"

Mr. Pennyfather held up a placating hand. "Oh, don't you worry. For him, it's definitely a punishment. His new office is at a dig near Bagdad. Mr. Evans is not a fan of the heat, dust, or rustic environments. Not to mention anything foreign."

All of which were present in plenty on such a dig site. I laughed at the thought of the fastidious man besieged by everything he loathed. "Why, you sly devil."

He dipped his head in acknowledgement.

"Who was the blond agent I saw you talking to at the museum? Was he in on it?"

Mr. Pennyfather shook his head. "He's clean. He was simply posing as a visitor to keep an eye on things and collect any evidence he could find."

"And Darrow and Foster?" I asked. "What's to happen to them?"

His expression turned grim. "It's best you don't ask. In fact, it's best you and your friends forget you ever met any of my agents or Dr. Foster. I am merely the husband of your aunt's dearest friend, and I am a simple bureaucratic cog in the great wheels of the British Empire."

A chill went down my spine. There was a threat in there, thinly veiled. "Agents? What agents?" I gave him a weak smile. "You're just a pencil pusher."

"Very good, my lady. Very good." He gave me a nod of approval, but his smile was rather like that of a shark.

We bid each other good day, and I could hardly wait to get out of there. Louise's rather bland husband was scary as the Devil himself. I did not ever want to cross that man.

Still, I paused before opening the door, turning to face him. "Interesting question. You didn't happen to have Darrow try and kidnap me, did you?"

He raised a brow. "Wouldn't need to, would I?"

"No, I suppose not. Although that's not really an answer, is it?"

He smiled that shark smile again. "Trust me, I had nothing to do with your kidnapping. That was all Darrow trying to throw you off the sent with a little help from his accomplice, Dr. Foster. Your reputation for tenacity proceeds you." It didn't sound like a compliment. "My understanding is that Darrow overheard me making the appointment with Louise and decided to take advantage. He didn't count on your cleverness or that you'd have assistance in the form of Mr. Singh."

I was afraid to ask how he knew about all of that, but it explained who the "old man" in the fake wig and beard was. "It wasn't Foster who tossed Mabel's flat though, was it?"

He shook his head. "That was Darrow. He was supposed to be staking out the place while I got a search team together. Instead, he decided to toss the place." He tapped the diary. "I guess he was outmatched."

I tried not to get too thrilled with the compliment. Such as it was. "Well… thank you, Mr.

Pennyfather. Have a lovely day. It's been nice… chatting."

I couldn't get out of that room fast enough. There aren't many people who make me uncomfortable, but Mr. Pennyfather had just moved to the top of the list.

I didn't breathe easy until I was out on the pavement in the sunshine. I took a deep breath of exhaust-fueled air as a car chugged by, embracing the clang of nearby roadworks and the shout of workers.

I was disappointed that the truth would be hidden, but justice would be served in her own way. Besides, Mabel hadn't struck me as the sort to care what anyone thought. In fact, as long as her work continued, she probably didn't give a toss what people said about her. And I'd have to settle for that, I supposed.

A familiar figured approached, a smile playing across handsome features. When he reached my side, Hale dropped a kiss on my lips. "How'd it go?"

"As well as could be expected." I glanced up at the dull, ordinary building that match the guise of its most important occupant. "Remind me never to cross Mr. Pennyfather."

"That bad?"

"He's more than he seems."

"Most people are, I've found."

I sighed. "That's certainly a fact."

"Ready for some lunch?"

My stomach rumbled. "I could eat." I could always eat. I was like my aunt in that way. "Aunt Butty will be crushed she won't be allowed to include this little adventure in her latest novel attempt." I slid my arm through the crook of Hale's as we strolled down the street.

"I imagine she'll get over it eventually," he said. "Or she'll figure out a way to squeeze it in without it being obvious."

"That's definitely more likely. Or at least she'll try. She's not really known for subtlety." I hoped she didn't get a visit from Mr. Pennyfather over it.

"How about you?" Hale asked. "Will you get over it? The fact that no one but us will ever know the truth?"

I mulled that over for a moment. "What is truth, anyway? Some can have truth thrown in their faces and never believe a word of it. And in this case, the truth might cause more harm than good. What Mr. Pennyfather and his men are doing is saving British lives."

"One bad apple can spoil the barrel," he pointed out.

"True, but the bad apples are being dealt with far better than the courts could manage." Darrow and Dr. Foster probably wished right about now they were in court instead of at Mr. Pennyfather's mercy. "As for Mr. Evans, well, that's just poetic justice. I can't think of a better punishment."

"And Mabel? I know you liked her."

I smiled. "She was... interesting. But I didn't really know her, did I? In the end, she was a conundrum. On the one hand, she was willing to put her life at risk to help MI5 stop the traitors from betraying us. On the other, she was willing to blackmail a couple of thieves just because she was angry the museum wouldn't fund her research. I get it, I really do. Sometimes being a woman and being treated as less than a man is quite... frustrating. I know you understand this more than anyone."

"I do," he agreed softly.

I squeezed his hand. "But what she did... well, that's just wrong. There is no excuse for it. She wasn't doing it to make the world a better place or because she was a suffragette or anything like that. She did it for selfish reasons and, in the end, she didn't care who got hurt by it. She may have been innocent of the thefts, and she may not have deserved being murdered, but I don't feel too badly about her getting blamed for those crimes since she can't answer for her true crimes."

"What about her the people she was investigating?" he asked.

"They're not yet sure who all is involved, but I turned over Mabel's diary to Mr. Pennyfather along with what I'd been able to decipher so far. He believes they'll be able to figure out who she was watching and stop them before any more harm is done."

He smiled. "I'm proud of you, you know."

"Really? Why?"

"You're good at this, love. Really good. You stopped the theft of important artifacts and more, you stopped a crooked agent and saved a lot of lives. Who knows how many in the long run."

I squeezed his arm. "Your support means the world to me, Hale."

"You've always supported me. I want to be there for you, too. Now come on, Chaz and James are stopping by for drinks later, but for now there's a new restaurant in Selfridges we should try." And he picked up the pace, hurrying us toward Oxford Street and the elegant edifice of the popular department store.

I grinned, hurrying to keep up, my arm still securely in his. Exactly where I wanted to be.

The End.

Want to know how Lady Rample got started solving mysteries?

Find out in the first Lady Rample Mystery, *Lady Rample Steps Out* available at online

retailers: https://books2read.com/u/4Aw2vk

Get free books and never miss a release by joining my
newsletter: https://www.sheamacleod.com/newsletter

When Lady Rample steps out, murder steps in.

*Lady Rample finds herself at odds after the death of her
husband until her best friend drags her to a hot new jazz club in
the heart of London. Before long, she finds herself embroiled in
the murder of one of the club's owners.*

*Bored with her aristocratic life and irked that the police have
arrested the wrong suspect, Lady R decides to turn lady
detective. With her eccentric Aunt Butty in tow, Lady R scours
London for clues. If she's lucky she'll find the killer before the killer
finds her.*

From the author of the Viola Roberts Cozy Mysteries comes the
first book in the Lady Rample Mysteries set in jazz-era London.

A Note from Shéa MacLeod

Thank you for reading. If you enjoyed this book, I'd appreciate it
if you'd help others find it so they can enjoy it, too.

Shéa MacLeod

Please return to the site where you purchased this book and leave a review to let other potential readers know what you liked or didn't like about the story.

Book updates can be found at www.sheamacleod.com

Be sure to sign up for my mailing list, so you don't miss out!
https://www.subscribepage.com/cozymystery

You can follow me on Facebook
https://www.facebook.com/sheamacleodcozymysteries
/ or on Instagram under @SheaMacLeod_Author. You can also find me on my website: https://www.sheamacleod.com/.

About Shéa MacLeod

Shéa MacLeod is the USA Today Best-Selling author of the *Lady Rample Mysteries*, the popular historical cozy mystery series set in 1930s London and the *Deepwood Witches Mysteries*. She's also written paranormal romance and mysteries, urban fantasy, and contemporary romances with a splash of humor. She resides in the leafy green hills outside Portland, Oregon, where she indulges her fondness for strong coffee, *Murder, She Wrote* reruns, vintage cocktails, and dragons.

Because everything's better with dragons.

Shéa MacLeod

Other Books by Shéa MacLeod

Lady Rample Mysteries
Lady Rample Steps Out
Lady Rample Spies a Clue
Lady Rample and the Silver Screen
Lady Rample Sits In
Lady Rample and the Ghost of Christmas Past
Lady Rample and Cupid's Kiss
Lady Rample and the Mysterious Mr. Singh
Lady Rample and the Haunted Manor
Lady Rample and the Parisian Affair
Lady Rample and the Yuletide Caper
Lady Rample and the Mystery at the Museum
Lady Rample and the Lady in the Lake

Sugar Martin Vintage Cozy Mysteries
A Death in Devon
A Grave Gala
A Christmas Caper
A Riviera Rendezvous

Viola Roberts Cozy Mysteries
The Corpse in the Cabana
The Stiff in the Study
The Poison in the Pudding
The Body in the Bathtub
The Venom in the Valentine
The Remains in the Rectory
The Death in the Drink
The Victim in the Vineyard
The Ghost in the Graveyard
The Larceny in the Luau

Edwina Gale Paranormal Investigator

Shéa MacLeod

(A Paranormal Women's Fiction Cozy Mystery Series)
Day of the Were-Jackal
Night of the Conjurer (coming soon)

Season of the Witch
(A Paranormal Women's Fiction Cozy Mystery Series)
Lifestyles of the Witch and Ageless
In Charm's Way
Witchmas Spirits
Battle of the Hexes

Intergalactic Investigations (SciFi Mysteries)
Infinite Justice
A Rage of Angels

Notting Hill Diaries (Sweet, Funny RomCom as Shéa R. MacLeod)
The Art of Kissing Frogs
To Kiss a Prince
Kiss Me, Chloe
Kiss Me, Stupid
Kissing Mr. Darcy

The Dream Factory (Women's Fiction/Magical Realism Co-Authored with Linda Mercury)
The Dream Factory
The Café of Hopes and Dreams
A Dream of Words

Printed in Great Britain
by Amazon